The Boy Barrier

D0725275

Jesse DuKore

SCHOLASTIC INC.
New York Toronto London Auckland Sydney

ISBN 0-590-33431-X

12 11 10 9 8 7 6 5 4 3 2 1   9   5 6 7 8 9/8 0/9

Printed in the U.S.A.   06

The Boy Barrier

A Wildfire Book

WILDFIRE® TITLES FROM SCHOLASTIC

One

She watched the solitary surfer crouching low on the sleek, burgundy-colored board. His wet blue-black hair glistened in the September sun. His bare arms, tanned and sinewy, were poised across the steadily rolling waves like a sea hawk about to spring into flight.

A navy jet screeched across the pale blue sky. But Stacey King only had eyes for the stranger, rooting for him as he and the board, one tightly-welded unit, skimmed on the crest of the curling waves. The perfect ride lasted only a moment. In that flicker of time, Stacey squinted into the sun, held her breath, and followed the flying young man.

Suddenly the wind kicked up and, with a great whoosh, a monster of a wave surged upward from the turbulent depths. The young man flew off, tumbling sideways into the Atlantic. The board barely missed his head as he lunged toward it. Moments later, the surfer and the board came together as the rough tide was pulled back out to sea. He threw his body over the long board and paddled heavily. Then he lay stomach-down and allowed a gentle wave to carry him to shore, away from Stacey.

"You couldn't get me out there in a million years," sighed Stacey to her best friend, Pam Hayward. "Oceans should be for fins and webbed feet only!"

She absent-mindedly brushed white sand from her cut-off jeans and stretched her freckled legs. Her big toe pointed toward the exhausted surfer trudging away from them, the battered board now over his head.

"Donny looks like one of those ladies down in the Bahamas," said Pam. "They can carry all kinds of heavy things on their heads. Ever see them?"

"No," admitted Stacey, "but I have a problem carrying all kinds of things INSIDE my head."

Stacey's joke masked a fleeting feeling of insecurity. Her friend knew so much about so many things.

Stacey knew about tennis; that world protected her from the realities of life. But it was a false protection. She was at an age where she was finally interested in developing relationships, and friendships with other girls. All her knowledge had been second-hand until recently. Pam was her first real friend. She wanted to know boys — and about boys, too. Her brother Michael was also a

2

good friend. But she knew it was time to get out into the world beyond her family, beyond tennis. This frightened and excited Stacey at the same time.

The two girls sat on their elbows and watched a young couple strolling hand in hand along the shore. A wistful sigh escaped Stacey's lips. There were so many questions that she wanted to ask her friend.

"I'm into the Bahamas," said Pam. "You know that's where my people are from, so I'm trying to find out what it's like there."

"Well, I'm sure it's warmer than northern Florida," said Stacey, "and I'll bet they don't have as many traffic jams on a Saturday night. See? You can ask me anything."

Pam waved to Donny. He waved back and motioned for her to come over. Stacey noted the exchange. She felt momentarily jealous of Pam's easy friendships with all the kids at school, something her own shyness prevented.

"Go on," said Stacey. "Go on over. I've got to work out this morning."

"It's Sunday, Miss King. A day of rest!"

"I find tennis very restful," Stacey answered, with a grin.

She scooped up a handful of sand, made a fist, and let the granules pour slowly out from the heel of her hand.

"You know," she confided in Pam, "I really can't imagine my life without tennis."

"Don't bet on it," said Pam, suddenly standing and stretching her tall, lanky frame.

"Hang around Pelican Beach and you'll discover the wonderful world of boys. You just might cut down your tennis diet to three hours a day."

"Four hours a day," declared Stacey. "No less. This year I'm going to win every state and regional tournament. And I think I'm ready for a national title."

"Wonderful," said Pam. "Terrific! When do you plan to do homework?"

"At night."

"And when do you plan to go out with boys?" asked Pam.

"I'm ready," declared Stacey. "Oh boy, am I ready! But I'm scared. Maybe I've just been talking to the wrong boys but it seems all they want to do is tell dumb jokes and play video games."

"And all *you* want to do is play tennis and win national titles," said Pam.

She looked over to Donny, who was now doing sit-ups, endlessly exercising. Without even thinking, Pam began swinging an imaginary tennis racquet.

"I love tennis almost as much as you do," continued the brown-skinned girl. "But there are more things in life than tennis, especially around here. Neptune goes in for the macho sports."

"I don't care what Neptune goes in for," argued Stacey. "I care about . . . what I care about."

"And you don't care about boys," said Pam. "At least not enough."

4

Stacey dug her heel into the sand, then kicked hard.

"Well," she said, "there are some attractive boys. . . . "

"Attractive, huh?" snorted Pam. "Hmph!"

The two friends giggled in a conspiratorial manner. Then Stacey's face turned serious. She put her head down and violently shook the sand out of her long brunette hair. Her braids swung like pendulums.

"I'm only fifteen," said Stacey. "I'll meet a boy — one of these days. I'll dazzle him with my freckled legs!"

Pam started to walk away backwards, still facing her friend.

"Oh come on, Stacey King. You don't know who you'll meet or what you'll do. You may be fifteen, but your life experience is pre-kindergarten. I'm sorry, maybe post-kindergarten."

Pam pointed a slim brown finger at Stacey, then pivoted on her bare feet and strode off. Stacey felt queasy. She didn't want to think about what Pam had said. She collected her big white towel, her tube of sun block, and her school books. Then she stood up and walked quickly to the near-empty parking lot, to her waiting bike. All Stacey wanted to do now was to get to the tennis courts and smack some balls.

It was September and the start of another school year at Neptune High School. The town of Neptune, on the northeastern coast of Florida, had a fishing fleet, a cannery, a naval air base, and a strong interest in football and baseball.

Stacey King played tennis. She was a slender, open-faced, attractive girl in her second year at Neptune High — the daughter of Bill and Lucinda King, who owned and operated the only pharmacy in town. From the age of eight Stacey had been encouraged to play tennis. The family goal, which became Stacey's goal, was for Stacey to become a nationally-ranked player — a champion, if possible. To achieve that end the dutiful, disciplined daughter had begun taking lessons with Lee Goodman, coach of the high school girls' tennis team. Summer vacations and holidays were for statewide tournaments.

Until she was eleven, Stacey would tremble slightly before the start of an important match. Because of her basic shyness, she never told anyone about the butterflies in her stomach. During the match and after every point, she would look over to her coach, her mother, her father, or her older brother Michael. She needed some sign of approval, of encouragement. Finally Lee Goodman had said, "If the game is no longer fun, you should quit or just make it a recreational sport. I don't want you to be unhappy. Tennis isn't that important."

Stacey stopped playing for six months. She felt like a fish out of water. The seventh grade was a time for parties and new girlfriends. She met Pam Hayward and Sally

Llewellyn and Bobbie Rose, her future team-mates at Neptune. These girls seemed so much older, so much wiser than she. The butterflies had returned to nest in her stomach during school hours and even after school. Finally, Stacey picked up a tennis racquet and resumed her lessons, her work-outs, and her tournaments. The butterflies had flown away.

When Stacey was ready to enter high school, the Kings wanted their daughter to attend school in Miami or Fort Lauderdale. The schools in the southern part of the state put more emphasis on competitive tennis. But Stacey turned out to be surprisingly strong-willed. She liked the small commu-nity of Neptune. She liked her grade-school friends. She wanted to play with them and continue to be coached by Lee Goodman. She saw no reason to uproot herself. Life was just fine the way it had always been.

And so, before the start of her second year at Neptune High, Stacey was convinced that her life would continue in the same, simple, easy-going way.

Late on that September afternoon, after her workout, Stacey sat in the section of the King Pharmacy where the high-school kids hung out in red-leather booths, huddled over formica tables, sipping sodas, and eating huge dishes of ice cream. She was drinking a tall glass of orange juice. She listened as Sally Llewellyn invited her to a mixed doubles match on Wednesday afternoon.

"It's going to be fun," Sally, a snub-nosed, bundle of energy, said. "You and Keith Flowers against me and Van Larsen. Big time, huh? Hot stuff!"

The two boys, both sixteen, were ranked first and second respectively on the Neptune boys' tennis team."

Stacey made a loud slurping noise as she sucked her orange juice through a straw.

"Sounds like a double date to me."

"Gosh," cried Sally, "haven't you ever played mixed doubles before? Boy — girl — boy — girl. It's not like you're going dancing at Hermosa Pier!"

"I'm not interested in mixed doubles," said Stacey. "I'm not even curious."

"I don't believe you," snapped Sally. "Anyway, even if you're not curious or interested in boys, you can bet your cutoff jeans that boys are going to be curious and interested in you!"

Stacey shook her head dramatically, as if she had just stepped out of a shower and was trying to dry her wet hair. But she was pleased by the compliment.

"What would some great-looking boy see in a fabulous beauty, sensational athlete, deep thinker, and dazzling dancer such as little ol' me?"

"Beats me," said Sally, grinning back at Stacey.

It was supposed to be social tennis, but on that breezy afternoon when Stacey walked onto the green asphalt court behind the high school, there were some interested spectators in the rickety old wooden grandstand. Two round-faced boys, identical twins, were sitting in the second row. Stan Jones (the older of the two brothers by some thirty minutes) nervously twiddled his thumbs as he watched Stacey begin serving in the opening game.

"She doesn't look like a tennis machine," he whispered to his brother.

Chuck Jones, whose face seemed to be in a constant grin, scratched his head with his left hand.

"She works out five or six hours a day," said Chuck. "She does roadwork, calisthenics — you name it, she does it. But she's a good looker . . . for a tennis machine."

Stan Jones scratched his short brown hair.

"Mind if I take her to the movies on Friday night?" he asked.

"Who am I?" shot back Chuck. "Her old man?"

Stacey served an ace against Van Larsen, who shook his head ruefully and walked slowly toward the net.

"Well," said Stan, "maybe you better go first. I'll feel better if you ask her. I mean, I'll feel easier if she turns *you* down."

"Thanks, brother," said Chuck.

Both twins watched enviously as their captain, the good-looking Keith Flowers, whispered advice to his new partner. Stacey listened and nodded her head like an attentive student.

The Jones boys were both on the Neptune tennis team and were impressed with Stacey's athletic ability. So was another person, sitting in the last row of the grandstand. He was a handsome, gray-haired man with sparkling blue eyes and a deeply-lined face from long hours in the sun. Hank Albertson, the coach of the boys' tennis team, was well aware of the talents of Keith Flowers and Van Larsen. But he was totally unprepared for Stacey King. During the course of the match, he began to move down toward the first row. Eventually, he wound up sitting alongside his friend, Lee Goodman.

"That young lady is . . . not bad," grudgingly admitted Hank Albertson. "She should have tougher competition."

Lee Goodman smiled confidently. "I've been telling you that for years," she said.

Stacey thought she was playing terribly. From her point of view, it was as if she was playing from memory. A voice inside her kept whispering, "Concentrate, just concentrate; keep your eyes on the ball." The reasons for Stacey's distraction were Keith Flowers and Van Larsen. Both boys were tall and handsome. Van, blond and steely blue-eyed, had a sarcastic wit. Just about every time Stacey made a great shot against him or Sally, he would yell across the net, "Not bad . . . for a girl." Keith Flowers, red-haired and quiet, was polite but withdrawn. He would clear his throat, approach Stacey with downcast eyes, and softly suggest that they "charge the net" at the same time.

Keith, like Stacey, was the number one player on his school team. Sally and Van were both ranked number two on their respective teams. With Sally and Van, there was a certain amount of bickering. After Van netted a hard hit ball from Stacey, Sally took him aside and hissed, "Can't you play more aggressively?" Van snapped back, "Keep on talking and I'll cancel Friday night!"

From where Stacey was playing, across the net, Van generated an intense animal magnetism that both attracted and frightened her. Keith, clearly the superior player, was moody and withdrawn. Nevertheless, he had a gentle quality that made Stacey feel warm and comfortable. Between the two of them and the intensity of the match, Stacey was emotionally drained.

Finally the last point was played on the windswept court. Sally hit a powerful overhead smash that seemed to be a clear winner. But Stacey, with her keen sense of anticipation, raced across court behind Keith Flowers and returned Sally's hard placement with a backhand shot straight down the line. Neither Sally nor Van had a chance to return it. Point — set — match went to the mixed doubles team of Stacey King and Keith Flowers. This time Van Larsen was too dumbstruck to make his typical wry remark. Sally mumbled under her breath, "From now on, Stacey can fix her own sweet, little-girl-self up with her own dates!" But, the next second, she was all smiles as she jogged to the net, reached across, and shook Keith's and Stacey's hands.

"Nice game, you two," smiled Sally.

Van Larsen said nothing. He simply nodded toward Stacey and pointed his racquet head at her. Keith broke into an uncharacteristic grin and winked at his new partner, then he walked off the court and was gone.

Hank Albertson rose and stretched his long arms.

"How's your number one player doing in the state tournaments?"

"She gets to the quarter-finals and semi-finals a lot," said Lee Goodman, "but she's not quite ready to go all the way. Something's missing. I don't know what it is."

Albertson saw the enormous potential of Stacey King. He was excited by what he had seen. There were ideas brewing in his head, but he said no more. He knew what was missing.

The world was changing radically in the eighties. If a woman could be vice-president of the United States, she could be . . . president of the United States. If a girl could play mixed doubles, why couldn't she play . . . mixed singles? Certainly this girl Stacey King had great possibilities that were not being realized. The girls' team was decent. But Stacey had power. She needed to be challenged . . . by boys! Then she would go all the way in her tournaments and start winning.

Albertson smiled quickly at no one in particular and walked away.

With a heavy sigh, Stacey collapsed on a bench and took a deep swig from her container of orange juice. She threw a white towel over her damp head and sat quietly, just trying to catch her breath. It had been a heady experience — a most unusual match.

"Nice playing," said Lee Goodman. "See you at practice tomorrow."

Stacey thought, Is that all she has to say? "Nice playing?" It didn't feel like "nice playing." But what had it felt like? She didn't know. Both Keith and Van had unnerved her in strange, unsettling ways. Her mind could not comprehend this new event. So Stacey tried to dismiss the boys from her mind. As before, she found refuge in the 78 feet-long-by-38-feet-wide rectangular court.

Yeah, she thought, I guess I did play well. Better than all right. And I guess I wasn't used to the high level of competition.

Now she was aware of a presence hovering around her. Someone was clearing his throat, over and over again. It was Chuck Jones from the boys' team.

"Hi. I'm Chuck. Chuck Jones?"

"I know," said Stacey, wiggling the toes inside her sneakers. "I've seen you play."

"Did you see my match against La Costa? My twin brother and I had some fun. We dressed exactly alike — white shorts, yellow shirts. I beat this guy in the first set and rushed back to the locker room. Then Stan came out and took the second set. Everybody from La Costa was amazed. 'Cause I took the first set playing lefty and Stan took the second set playing righty. They thought I was a . . . phenomenon!"

Stacey laughed, then began collecting her three racquets and putting them into her tennis bag. She stood up.

"Ummm, excuse me," said Chuck. "I was wondering if you'd like to get together some time, like Friday night? Unless you have other plans?"

Stacey nodded her head. So this is what it was like, she thought. I wonder if every boy is nervous when he asks a girl to go out. Or is it me, *making* him nervous?

Chuck continued rambling in a jaunty, jolly manner, telling another tennis anecdote. Stacey listened politely as she continued to walk toward her bike. She was flustered. It was her first date with an upperclassman.

That night, Stacey called Pam and told her about her upcoming date with Chuck Jones. She claimed to be looking forward to it.

"You don't sound very excited," said Pam. "Well, Chuck is not exactly Mister Thrill-A-Minute. But he's a nice guy. If you don't mind listening to his endless stories. Just laugh every two minutes and he'll be happy."

That Friday night at Hermosa Pier, Stacey did not laugh every two minutes. But she knew enough to act pleasantly, to smile, to listen attentively. It wasn't easy. Chuck Jones had a habit of talking endlessly, of rambling, of thinking himself the funniest storyteller in the world. As a result, he didn't leave much room for Stacey to participate. Even though she didn't know how to dance, Stacey welcomed the dancing. The music was loud enough that Chuck could barely shout above the noise. Finally he gave up. Stacey enjoyed the band, and was even able to enjoy her partner as she both followed him and improvised steps. But somehow something was missing. Many hours later, they left the pier after mutually acknowledging that their feet were killing them.

She said goodnight at the front door. Then Chuck shut his eyes as if he was in pain — and tried to kiss her. Stacey backed off nervously. The gentle sound of the door closing in Chuck's face got his eyes open. Stacey, on the other side of the door, breathed a sigh of relief.

A short time later, Chuck told his brother that Stacey King was indeed Miss Tennis Machine.

Stacey sat by her bedroom window looking across the row of mimosas and palm trees, wondering if every boy would be like Chuck Jones. Or maybe she would have to learn about dating the way she learned about tennis — from practice. Her head began to ache. It was all too much to think about. She never had trouble talking with Pam or Sally or even her brother Michael. Her tennis was getting better. Why shouldn't her dating technique get better? She had to start somewhere. Chuck Jones represented her first baby steps.

But when Stacey finally got into bed, she began to think back to that Wednesday mixed-doubles match. As she drifted off into a dreamless sleep, she saw herself dancing at Hermosa Pier with Keith Flowers. The lights flashed and the music grew louder, as Keith whirled her around and around. Soon, she was fast asleep.

On Sunday afternoon, Stacey went for a long run along Pelican Beach with Sally Llewellyn. Sandpipers scurried out of their path. Terns swooped overhead. Stacey confessed that she had been petrified on her Friday night date.

"Chuck Jones behaved like a perfect gentleman. . . . "

"Whatever *that* means!" snickered Sally.

". . . but I just didn't know what to say or what to do. Maybe I'm playing too much tennis," cried Stacey.

"You want to take another shot at mixed doubles?" asked Sally. "You owe us a rematch."

"No way," said Stacey, immediately regretting her words.

Right then and there, Sally decided to do something about the innocent Stacey King.

Two

"Come on, you guys! Who's going to hit with me?"

It was five o'clock on a humid afternoon as Stacey stood alongside the team bench. Her Neptune High T-shirt was dripping wet. A blister was developing inside her thumb. Again, she pleaded for one sparring partner.

Lee Goodman turned to the grandstand and winked at Hank Albertson. Her eyes indicated amusement and pride in her number one player. Albertson, a now frequent observer of Stacey, simply shrugged his shoulders.

"See you next week, Lee," said the gentle-voiced Albertson. "I want to check out your star pupil in action against tougher competition."

"The girls from the Del Ray School are pretty tough," said Lee. "But Stacey will do fine, just fine."

Albertson stood up and stretched his long arms. In his right hand, he held a notebook. During the workout, he'd been making notes on various aspects of Stacey's game.

"We'll see," he said quietly. "They've got a new girl from Mexico City, Maria Torres, who's played on the international circuit. I hear she's beating everybody."

"Time to quit," barked Lee Goodman. "You, too, Miss King. Take a break. Do some homework. I don't want you flunking out of school."

Pam, Sally, and Bobbie Rose burst out laughing. Stacey simply shifted from one leg to the other. She was not amused.

"No way I'm going to flunk out," said Stacey.

"Well," said Sally, "if you do, I'm ready to take your place."

Lee Goodman adjusted the visor of her navy blue baseball cap against the rays of the glaring sun.

"See you all tomorrow," she said. "Practice at two. And don't forget next Monday. Del Ray's going to be tough."

Sally, Bobbie, and Pam headed for the showers.

"How about you, Pam?" asked Stacey. "Just another half-hour?"

Pam took a deep breath. Then, with a couple of comic strides, like a weary marathon runner approaching the finish line, she was beside her friend.

"Enough, Stacey. Enough. You've worn out

the entire Neptune squad. You've worn out the coach. Now listen, King, there's more to life than hitting a fuzzy yellow ball with a racquet made out of nylon strings."

"I know that," said Stacey, defensively. "Anyway, I don't use nylon. I use lamb's gut."

Stacey giggled, a tell-tale sign that she was aware of her absurdity.

"I don't care if you use polyester fiber," shouted Pam. "I'm going home. I'm not even going to think about any big matches against Del Ray or anybody else. See you."

Pam gathered her tennis racquets and ran after her teammates, who were headed for the shower room. Stacey watched them for a moment, then picked up a wire basket of tennis balls and walked slowly to the base line of the court. There was a grim, resolute expression on her face as Stacey worked on her serve, over and over again, tossing the ball forward and over her right shoulder in a high arc. For the next forty minutes, she repeated this exercise, even as the afternoon sun cast a long shadow across the court. Neither the glaring sun nor the humid afternoon deterred Stacey from this disciplined drill. Finally, when the blister on her thumb cried out for attention, she said aloud, "Okay, Stace, time to call it a day. A day!"

The Kings lived in a white stucco house with orange shutters and a red-tiled roof in the old Spanish style. It was a small but comfortable home, surrounded by lush vegetation — palmettoes and mimosa trees out front and on either side of the quarter-acre plot. Behind the house was a manicured green lawn, an avocado tree, and a lemon tree. It was the kind of house that a tourist might see in the south of France, in Spain, or in Mexico. What gave the King home its distinctive quality was the canal that bordered the back yard. On weekends tiny fishing boats slowly drifted past on their way out to sea. But on weekday nights Stacey would sit on the stone wall and let her feet dangle over the quiet waters. Sometimes, a boat would glide by, its outboard motor making a putt-putt noise. The owner, off for a few hours of night fishing, might wave at Stacey — sometimes she would wave back.

On this particular Wednesday night Mr. and Mrs. King were away for their weekly bridge game, Michael was practicing a Brahms piece on his violin, and Stacey had some unexpected guests. It was eight o'clock when Sally and Bobbie Rose showed up at the front door.

"Hey, how're you guys doing?" cried Stacey. "Have some fresh oranges to celebrate this unexpected pleasure."

She skipped over to a wide glass bowl, reached in and began tossing oranges to the two girls. They each caught three, then begged off as the shiny fruit hit them and rolled onto the carpet.

"Enough, Stacey," said Sally. "We already

appreciate your hospitality. One orange will do."

Stacey smiled. She was so glad her friends had stopped by. Their visit was a welcome relief from studying chemistry.

"There's such a nice breeze off the canal tonight," she said. "Let's go outside."

"So how do you like the new windsurfing instructor?" asked Stacey after they were settled. "Max Vogel, that college student from Germany. I think he's only nineteen or twenty years old."

"He's adorable," sighed Bobbie Rose. "But his pretty blond head is so thick. What do you think of him?"

"I don't mind his head," said Stacey. "He's a great teacher. He's got me flying all over the ocean. I hardly ever fall off. And I'm learning to go against the wind." She sighed with pleasure. "Did you ever notice that Max can't pronounce 'tacking.' It comes out 'tocking,' as in tic-tocking," Stacey continued.

"Sounds like you've got a little crush on him," said Sally.

Stacey's blush was not lost on the two girls. She turned away and reached for an orange.

"I appreciate a good instructor," said Stacey. "And like I said, he's made me a good windsurfer."

She paused to peel the skin off the orange, then took a big bite.

"And like I didn't say," said Stacey, between mouthfuls of the juicy fruit, "he's definitely cute."

"But he speaks with marbles in his mouth," Bobbie Rose snickered.

Before Sally added her own sarcastic remark to top Bobbie's, Stacey cleared her throat and asked if either girl wanted some lemonade.

Bobbie's eyes lit up. She opened her mouth and raised her index finger, as if signalling a waiter, but Sally cut her off.

"We just stopped by to invite you to a party this coming Saturday night. Bobbie's folks let her have the house."

"I'll be there," said Stacey. "Thanks."

Bobbie stood on the stone wall and balanced herself like a gymnast. She stood erect on the balls of her feet and extended her arms toward the water.

"Hey, Bobbie Rose," said Sally, "you're going to fall in the water. Then what do we do about a house for the party?"

"Oh yeah, one thing," said Bobbie Rose, trying to ignore her friend's remarks, "it's a B.Y.O.B. party."

There was a moment of silence, interrupted by the chirping of invisible crickets. Finally, Sally spoke up. "What's the problem?"

"I don't drink," explained Stacey.

There was another long silence.

"I don't get it," said Sally, sitting on the edge of the canal wall.

"My brother's gone to those parties," said Stacey, "and he doesn't like them."

"Whoa now," said Bobbie, jumping down

off the wall. "What do you think a B.Y.O.B. party is?"

Now both girls were sitting cross-legged on the grass as Stacey paced back and forth. Fireflies darted swiftly in front of their eyes. The cricket sounds were shattering the silence. Stacey sat down heavily, facing her teammates.

"Bring your own bottle," she answered.

The squeals and the laughter of Sally and Bobbie drowned out the crickets. Now Stacey was grinning self-consciously.

"What did I say?" she asked.

"B.Y.O.B.," said Sally, "means Bring Your Own Boy."

There was another long silence. Suddenly the back door opened and a tall, stoop-shouldered young man was standing there, clutching a violin. It was Michael. He waved to the girls with his violin bow.

"Hey, Michael," shouted Bobbie, "can you play any country music?"

"Sure," said the amiable Michael. "What country would you like to hear?"

"Hah hah hah," said Stacey, in a rare sarcastic tone.

Michael tucked the instrument under his chin and began to play "Tennessee Waltz." He continued to stand by the back door.

Michael King practiced his violin music as much as Stacey practiced her tennis. He had already given concerts throughout the state. He was in the eleventh grade at Neptune High. His dream was to study music at Juilliard in New York City. It was considered the finest music school in the country.

But now, while crickets chirped and a fishing boat grunted past, Michael was having a good time playing for his sister and her friends, doing what he called "a little country fiddlin'." When he finished, the girls applauded, Michael bowed low, then stretched his skinny arms to acknowledge the applause, turned, and re-entered the house.

There was another long silence.

"So what's the problem?" asked Sally.

She sounded more exasperated than concerned. Sally and Stacey were friendly without being friends. Tennis was their common bond. And, for Sally Llewellyn, there was a curiosity as to what made Stacey tick, what made her such an aggressive tennis player, yet so naive off the court.

"I don't have any boy to bring to the party," sighed Stacey.

"What about the Joneses?" asked Bobbie. "Which one did you date, Chuck or Stan?"

"Whichever one it was," said Sally, "I heard it was a real bomb. Seems he spoke about you as being a 'Tennis Machine.'"

Stacey gasped. A dull pain pierced her chest, right smack in the center. She could feel her eyes begin to tear and her throat go dry.

"It was Chuck," she said, finally. "The lefty."

Sally stood up, followed by Bobbie Rose.

They couldn't see Stacey's eyes clearly under the overcast night sky. But they did sense that she was upset.

"Well," said Bobbie Rose, "maybe you ought to try the righty. I heard that Stan has a good sense of humor."

"Who'd you hear it from?" asked Sally.

"From Chuck," replied Bobbie Rose.

The two girls laughed quickly as they strolled across the lawn. Stacey remained, cross-legged, on the grass.

"If you find a boy," called out Sally, "bring him to the party. Oh, and I strongly recommend that you do something about those braids."

Stacey tugged at her tightly-knit braids with both hands tightly clenched. Her head ached from the tugging.

"I am not a tennis machine," she mumbled.

But Sally and Bobbie Rose were gone.

She called to her brother, but he had resumed practicing and couldn't hear her.

"I am not a tennis machine," she repeated. "Just 'cause I love to practice long hours doesn't make me a machine. Besides, they're just jealous. Sally's number two and Bobbie Rose is number three, and Chuck Jones is . . . is. . . . "

Michael was standing in the frame of the back door. His sensitive eyes looked down on his kid sister, trying to make sense of her tear-splattered face.

"Only people with lots of money in the

bank talk to themselves," he said. "At least that's what Dad used to tell me."

"Why?" asked Stacey. "Did you used to talk to yourself?"

"I still do," laughed Michael, "when I practice. I'll say, 'Oh boy, that was a clinker' or 'Not bad for a beginner.' Sometimes I'll even say, 'Not bad.'"

"Don't talk to yourself when you're giving concerts in New York City," said Stacey.

Michael put his arm around Stacey's shoulders and guided her toward the canal. The air was filled with the scent of the lemon tree. In the sky, the north star was suddenly visible.

"So why are you talking to yourself?" asked Michael. "And why the tears?"

Stacey stretched out full-length on the stone wall. She began chewing on the tip of her left braid.

"Do you think I practice too much?" she asked.

"Hey, don't ask me," answered Michael. "I'm a practice nut. Sometimes I practice so much I forget to eat. Hey, come on, Stace, what's going on? What did those girls say to upset you?"

"Oh, it's not important," mumbled Stacey.

"Of course not," said Michael with a slight chuckle.

Stacey sighed. The sigh came from deep within her aching chest right on up through her dry throat.

"I really do love tennis," she said, finally.

Michael studied her sweet face. His little

sister sometimes had the biggest eyes in the world. And this tough little tennis player, one of the best in the whole state of Florida, could sometimes have the most helpless expression.

"Let me tell you something about myself," said Michael. "I had a real crush on a cellist named Donna. But I figured she'd never go out with me because I was so skinny and puny and funny-looking and. . . . "

"You're not puny," said Stacey.

She paused like a professional comedian.

"Just skinny and funny-looking," Stacey said before cracking up.

Michael roared like a wounded lion, then picked up his sister and made believe he was going to dump her into the canal. Stacey shrieked. He dropped her gently back on the wall.

"Anyway," continued Michael, "she turned me down when I asked her for a date. So I played my violin twice as hard and twice as long. I was really miserable. Then, one day, I met a cellist named Roberta. . . . "

"Boy, you've really got a thing for cellists."

"Well," said Michael, "you know Roberta. She's great. And she doesn't care that I'm funny-looking and skinny or that I practice a lot. In fact, she likes me precisely for those reasons."

Stacey rolled over and landed on the soft grass.

"So what's the point of the story?" she cried out in a mock-serious voice. "A story's got to have a punch line. What's your punch line? Come on. Be snappy."

Michael stood up and shoved his hands deep into the pockets of his khaki trousers.

"I didn't change," he said. "I kind of liked who I was and how I looked and what I did. I didn't know it at the time but it happened that somebody came along — Roberta — who liked me for all the reasons that Donna didn't like me. So the point is: Be yourself and somebody will come along who'll like the fact that you play tennis four or five hours a day, seven days a week."

"Will he like my braids?" asked Stacey.

"I don't know."

"Will he mind that I'm a crummy dancer?" she asked.

"Not everybody's a good dancer," said Michael. "Look at me."

He hugged her tightly, tapped her playfully on the head, then kissed her on both cheeks.

"I still have to find a boy for Saturday night," said Stacey.

"You mean you can't come to the party if you don't have a date?"

"Yeah."

"That's ridiculous," said Michael. "Girls don't usually ask boys to go to a party. I'll bet there'll be lots of girls without dates."

"You think so?"

"Or maybe I can find you a date," suggested Michael.

"Don't you dare," shrieked Stacey. "Anyway, maybe I should do something about my braids. Maybe I should do something about learning to. . . . "

Suddenly she began to yawn. Over and over again, her mouth opened wide and a deep, moaning sound escaped.

"Well," sighed Stacey, "it was nice of Bobbie and Sally to invite me, even if I am a tennis machine."

"Let's go inside, kid."

"You go ahead," said Stacey. "I'll just be a few minutes."

She lay down on the grass, breathing the scent of fresh lemons. She knew that she wasn't a machine. She knew she had strong feelings — toward the game she loved so much, toward her family, toward her friends, especially Pam Hayward. It was mean of Chuck Jones to use that terrible expression. And it was mean of Sally Llewellyn to repeat those words. Well, thought Stacey, people are funny. Maybe Sally was just upset because of her fight with Van Larsen. At least she's got someone to fight with, Stacey mused.

She closed her eyes and tried to imagine what she would look like without braids. She tried to picture herself with flowing hair, gliding around a dance floor, dancing at Bobbie Rose's house. She tried to get a glimpse of the kind of special boy who might not mind dancing with a . . . with a hard-driving tennis player. Again, her mind drifted to the handsome face of Keith Flowers.

When Bill and Lucinda King drove up the

driveway, the headlights of their car illuminated the sleeping figure of their daughter. As Mrs. King turned off the ignition, Mr. King got out of the car, hurrying to his daughter's side.

"You okay, honey?"

Stacey woke up and smiled at her father's face. Then she realized where she was and stood up suddenly.

"Hi, Dad, hi, Mom. Guess I fell asleep."

She walked drowsily into the white stucco house — still lost in a dream of dancing with Keith Flowers. But when Stacey crawled into bed, she was suddenly wide-awake. There was no longer any Keith nor was there music. If Stacey had been dubbed a tennis machine, there had to be a reason. Didn't Pam call her pre-kindergarten? Who else had braids in the tenth grade? Who else practiced a sport so many hours a day? Who else didn't know any boys well enough to ask to a B.Y.O.B. party? Who else began to perspire and tremble when she had to dance? Had to dance!

Stacey wanted to dance, wanted to look lovely, wanted to know how to go out with boys. If she really was a tennis machine, then Stacey King had better do something about it . . . if she could!

Three

On Saturday night Stacey showed up at Bobbie Rose's house with a new look, but not with a new boy. Her braids were gone, replaced by a soft, longish look. Her brunette hair was gently pulled back and tied with a pink bandanna. She wore white jeans with a navy blue T-shirt. To Stacey's uncomplicated way of thinking, her outfit was attractive and comfortable, and she rather liked her new hair style.

Bobbie Rose opened the door. Her hair was piled up in curls. She wore lipstick and eyeliner.

"Hey, Bobbie, you sure look tall!" Stacey looked down and saw that her hostess was wearing three-inch heels.

"You sure look small," exclaimed Bobbie Rose.

Stacey was wearing tennis shoes.

Pam, Stacey, and a trio of girls from the

swimming team came out. They were also wearing fancy outfits, makeup, and high heels. Pam looked at Stacey and shook her head critically.

"Oh well, Stacey, come on in," she moaned.

"Thanks," said Stacey, mortified by the fashion show before her.

The spacious living room was cleared for dancing. The Jones brothers were sitting in a corner, laughing uproariously at something in a magazine. Van Larsen was there, looking through a collection of records. The boys all looked up when Stacey entered the room.

"Hi, guys," she said, smiling lamely.

"You look like you're still dressed for school," Van said sarcastically.

"Oh shut up, Larsen," said Pam. "Just find some good dancing music."

All the girls were wearing flashy blouses, designer jeans, and jewelry. And it became evident, as the painfully long evening wore on, that all the girls had dates. Stacey felt like a little kid, a misfit with two left feet, two left hands, and a tongue that could only babble on about . . . tennis. Nobody told her she actually *had* to bring a boy!

Everyone was nice to her, which made Stacey even more uncomfortable. Now she felt like an extraterrestrial, an alien creature, whom every one had vowed to make feel at home. Chuck Jones danced with Stacey. Then, of course, Stan Jones danced with her. Van Larsen took her aside and volunteered to teach her a few steps.

"I guess you don't listen to the radio much," he whispered loudly, "but this is what we're dancing to these days, here on earth. Just relax your body."

"It's relaxed; it's relaxed," she protested. "It's a human body!"

Of course she felt tight as a drum. And something was missing. Someone was missing. Stacey's mind didn't seem to function. When Keith Flowers entered the noisy room, she realized that he had been the missing element. When she looked again she realized he was with a striking, dark-haired girl named Debby Klinger.

"Hi, Keith."

"Hi, Stacey."

"How'd you do against Ponte Vedra?"

"We lost," said Keith, without any emotion.

"How'd *you* do?"

"I won," he said, simply.

Stacey was impressed. Then she nodded in the direction of Debby Klinger.

"Your girl friend's gorgeous."

"Yeah," said Keith. "She works at it."

The long-legged Debby was dancing with a husky young man named Alex. When the frantic beat was replaced with a slow Latin rhythm, Debby turned and began dancing with Stan Jones.

"Don't you like to dance?" asked Stacey, not without some trepidation.

"Sometimes," answered Keith, "but not

when I'm uncomfortable. No point in pushing it."

Stacey was afraid to ask what the "it" was that Keith didn't want to push. But she felt easy standing there with him, watching the others dance.

The worst part of the evening was yet to come. As all the couples were leaving (Bobbie Rose's parents came home precisely at midnight), Stacey stepped outside into the warm Florida night and there was Michael, standing by his old green convertible.

"Hiya kid," shouted Michael, "here's your escort service."

"Yeah, thanks," mumbled Stacey. "Just what I need."

Between her "school outfit," the absence of a date, and the presence of her cheery, responsive brother, Stacey would have liked an escort service . . . out of town!

They drove along Pelican Parkway with the top down on the Chevrolet.

"I'm fifteen, going on adolescence," moaned Stacey, her face tilted upward to the midnight sky. "I'm at least three or four years behind my girl friends. Got to play catch-up."

"I disagree," argued Michael. "You can never play catch-up. What does Lee Goodman always say to you? You can only play your game, moment to moment."

"Don't drive so fast," cried Stacey.

"Don't change the subject," Michael said, slowing down. A huge truck roared past them, flying north. The driver tooted the small convertible out of the way with a harsh whistle.

"I think you're just shy," Michael said. "Nothing wrong with that."

"Well," said Stacey, "I'm really *not* shy. I just never thought of boys and . . . and clothes and boys . . . that sort of thing. Now I'm thinking."

"Me, too," said Michael.

"Oh, you? You're always thinking."

"No, I mean I've been thinking about you," explained Michael. "I think maybe I should fix you up with a friend of mine."

"Uh oh," muttered Stacey.

The green Chevrolet slowed down as they drove past the deserted fruit and vegetable markets. Soon they were heading back toward the narrow bridge that spanned the Kaufman Canal.

Michael cleared his throat. He began to whistle a light Mozart piece for violin. Stacey straightened her back, then stretched her arms to the night sky. Her fingers caught the warm breeze.

"Okay, brother, let's have it. I always know when you're ready to make a great pronouncement."

He slowed down as they crossed the bridge. Immediately the neighborhood changed, the shanty town of the immigrants was behind them. Now there were only neat lawns and white homes.

"I know this really great guy," began

Michael. "His name is Wally Baxter."

"The football star. I've seen him."

Stacey tried to affect a bored, sophisticated air. But her neck was perspiring. And her lower back was getting tense.

"Stace, you're not a little girl anymore. You have to make room for a social life. Boys can be fun. Hah hah hah!"

"Are you sure boys can be fun? I know you can be fun. I know Dad can be fun, even though he's not exactly a boy. Everybody else, I'm not so sure about."

She thought of Chuck Jones. He hadn't been much fun; certainly not the barrel of laughs he'd tried to be. The face of Keith Flowers popped into her head. She tried to dismiss the image.

"I guess I can learn to get along with boys," Stacey mused. "I'd like to — very much. I'm just . . . scared."

"Get along with . . . ?" began Michael as he slowed down and brought the car into the driveway.

"Go along with," sighed Stacey. "Go out with — and dress up for — and dance up . . . a storm. And I really can dance up a storm. Oh well, you know what I mean. You *do* know what I mean, don't you?"

"Yeah," said Michael. "I know what you mean."

Four

Anyone watching Stacey King on that Friday morning would never suspect she had a big match on Friday afternoon. Her long, gleaming hair, tied with a bright yellow ribbon, bounced up and down as she walked quickly and easily to her first class of the day: computer science. It was an unseasonably cool morning so she wore the team jacket that read "Neptune Tennis." All during the class she was attentive, working well at the keyboard, taking notes when it was necessary. At ten minutes to nine, she chatted briefly with Julia De Diego and Bridget Wood. They laughed lightly as a trio of "muscle boys" paraded past in a state of constant flexing.

"Hey, Bridget," whispered Stacey, "I hear that pumping iron is a big thing with girls. When are you going to start working out?"

"When you do, I will," replied the red-headed Bridget.

"You don't want to do that," said Julia, a recent arrival from Honduras. "All that muscle turns to flan."

Bridget and Stacey burst out laughing.

"The word is flab," said Stacey. "Flan is something you eat for dessert . . . as if you didn't know, wise guy!"

The three girls quickened their pace so they would be on time for their world history class. As Stacey was about to enter the classroom, she spied Keith Flowers.

"Hey," shouted Keith, "good luck today."

"Oh, thanks," said Stacey, feeling her heart beating a little quicker.

"What's happening today?" asked Bridget, as they all found their seats.

"We're playing the kids from Del Ray," said Stacey, nonchalantly.

That was the end of that. There were no follow-up questions from either Bridget or Julia, no particular desire or curiosity to know more about the match, and that was just fine with Stacey. She was not out to impress them. She didn't need anyone's approval. She was totally secure on a tennis court. It was the fleeting appearance of Keith, his sincere expression, that stayed with Stacey and disturbed her, even as she felt warm and good.

At twelve o'clock Stacey jogged to the number one court with her tennis racquets tucked under her arm. She ate a hard-boiled egg and an orange. She practiced with Pam for thirty minutes, hitting the ball easily and loosening her muscles, then, on to chemistry.

Two hours later, she was back, ready to play. By this time, the Del Ray tennis squad was practicing on the two far courts. There were eight girls, all engaged in a serious work-out. Stacey was now feeling the nervous excitement that always accompanied the start of a big match. Her opponent, Maria Torres, had a national reputation as a promising junior player. In her native Mexico, she was ranked number one. As a new American and a recent Floridian, Maria Torres was already number two in the state.

"Okay, kids," said Lee Goodman, as her players formed a semicircle around her. "Go out there and win this one for Neptune."

All the girls burst out laughing and clapped their hands, except Stacey who shook her head and frowned.

"But seriously," continued the coach, "I want all of you to just play steadily. In this kind of match, the player who gets the ball over the net the most times wins. Steadiness is the name of the game. Let them try all the flashy stuff they want."

"It's kind of breezy out there, coach," said Stacey. "Might be hard to stay back and rally."

"A good point," said Lee. "But don't try any aggressive net play unless your opponent hits a short ball. Okay? Okay!"

Stacey removed her warm-up pants. As she

did so, she noticed that Keith Flowers was, at that very moment, sitting in the back row behind the net. A gray-haired man, wearing a white shirt and tie was sitting next to him. She recognized the man as Hank Albertson, coach of the boys' team.

"We have some celebrities here today," said Stacey to Pam.

Pam checked them out, then grinned.

"How's my hair, Ms. King?"

"Delightfully luxurious," said Stacey, adjusting her yellow bow.

Pam pretended to gag as she screwed up her lovely face.

"Girl, you've been watching much too much television," she exclaimed.

When Stacey stepped onto the court for the brief warm-up, she concentrated totally on the fuzzy yellow ball. Keith receded to the back of her mind. Even her opponent's reputation faded away — the hours of training all came to the forefront. Stacey did not try to play any differently than she had in the mixed doubles or in her practice matches with Pam. She simply played her game. Two hours and twenty minutes later, she had defeated Maria Torres, 7-5, 7-5, 6-4. It had been a difficult match. The rallies had been long and exciting for both girls. When it was over they ran quickly toward the net, shook hands, nodded to the referee in the high chair, and walked off the court.

Stacey sat on the bench, put on her jacket, and draped a towel over her head. All the nervous energy had been drained from her. She felt hollow.

"Well, you did it, kid," said Lee Goodman. "In fact, you were the only one who did it. Sally is in the process of getting whipped on the number two court. And Bobbie Rose and Pam were pretty soundly thrashed on the number three court. So — it was a great day for you and another step backward for Neptune. Oh well, it's just a game. Although it would be nice if we won some team matches from time to time."

Stacey slumped forward on the bench. She had heard these words before. Coach Goodman was resigned to the inferior play of the squad. Stacey was frustrated; she wanted more from her teammates. But the girls had no intense desire either to win or improve their game. Lee Goodman was simply grateful that she was able to get four bodies out onto the courts to represent the school.

"Good game, Stacey."

Suddenly Keith Flowers was standing there in front of her. The sun was breaking through the dark purple sky, creating a nimbus behind Keith's soft red hair. Stacey had to squint to see the smile on his face.

"Glad you could make it," she said. "It was a good match."

"Yeah," he agreed. "Hey, maybe we can get in some mixed doubles again. Or even play singles."

"Any time," said Stacey, without thinking. She was too tired, too drained to be excited by Keith's presence. His presence confused Stacey. She didn't understand the message, if there was one, coming from him. Did he just want to play some social tennis? Or serious tennis? Or was Keith a retiring guy who didn't know how to ask a girl out?

Doesn't seem likely, thought Stacey. He always has a girl around.

A moment later, Debby Klinger was calling Keith's name from the grandstand.

"Well," said Keith, looking at Stacey intently and barely acknowledging Debby's presence, "see you 'round."

"Yeah," said Stacey, too exhausted to look up again, "see you 'round."

If Stacey had looked all the way around to the top row of the grandstand, she would have seen Coach Goodman in a huddle with Hank Albertson. As they spoke in hushed voices, they were concentrating on Stacey as she walked slowly to the locker room.

"She's good," said Albertson, poking his thick index finger in the direction of Stacey. "The girl plays a real power game. She can go all the way. Number one in the state. A national ranking. Could even turn pro some day — and some day soon."

"Yeah," said Lee Goodman. "If she was down in Fort Lauderdale or Miami, she'd have a national reputation. Neptune doesn't know what a prize it has. The other girls would rather be windsurfing or dancing. I suppose I should be grateful that at least they put in the hours, even without the spirit."

"Know what you mean," agreed Albertson. "Coaching tennis here is like starting a bowling club in Tahiti."

"Who in their right mind would start a bowling club in Tahiti?" asked Lee Goodman.

"Now you've got it!"

Twenty minutes later, the two coaches were still talking as Stacey emerged from the clubhouse. She was wearing a bright orange T-shirt, white jeans, and an old pair of sneakers. Around her firm shoulders was the Neptune tennis jacket.

The girls from Del Ray had taken quick showers and were already back in their cars and vans, heading home. Pam, Bobbie Rose, and Sally were still hanging out in the locker-room talking. Stacey just stood there, her racquet bag slung over her shoulder. In her right hand, she clutched a small duffel bag that contained her damp tennis clothes and her school books. The bag felt like it weighed a ton.

"Lee," began Hank Albertson, looking over in Stacey's direction, "that girl is not realizing her full potential with these matches. Not enough competition. No big challenges. Oh sure, that Maria Torres is good. But Stacey King needs to play with tougher players all the time. She ought to be out there with heavy hitters, every day, to raise the level of her game."

"You've got something on your mind," said Lee. "Come on, I know you. You've been talking around the subject for several weeks now. Spit it out."

Stacey was walking toward her bike.

"I propose," said Hank Albertson, "that Stacey King . . . join the boys' tennis team."

Lee stood up. The idea was shocking — but it made sense. Instinctively she knew that her friend was right. Still, it was disturbing. The repercussions would be felt by everyone — the girls, the school, the town. It was a radical idea whose time had come.

"If we're going to talk any further about this, we'd better include the subject. . . . I'll go catch her."

Lee Goodman needed to get away, to run. She always thought best when she was on the move. Now, as she ran slowly toward her star player, her mind was racing. The loss of Stacey would make no appreciable difference to the girls' squad. It was still a losing team. There were some promising ninth-graders who could be brought in, even if they weren't quite ready. What did it mean to be ready? Ready to lose? Maybe the new blood would turn the team around? Maybe Sally Llewellyn, who would now be number one, would thrive on her new status. Perhaps Stacey King had been an intimidating factor. Subconsciously the other players might have resented the no-nonsense presence of Stacey King. Hank Albertson's idea might benefit everyone.

"Stacey, wait a second," shouted Lee.

"Let's take a little walk across the road," said Hank. "I like to look at the ocean around this time. Very restful."

It was almost six o'clock. The light flashed green and Stacey, Hank, and Lee crossed the parkway. They made their way to a white wooden bench that faced the sun-tinted water.

"Okay," said Lee, "I suppose you're wondering what this seaside meeting is all about?"

"Well," said Stacey, "I'm not kidding myself. I know there's lots of room for improvement. And I guess I made some mistakes. . . . "

"Young lady," said Albertson. "You didn't make any mistakes. The reason for this seaside meeting is that I want you to join the boys' tennis team."

Lee smiled and said, "You don't have to answer right away."

Stacey pushed the canvas bag onto the sand, then she looked out to the turbulent ocean. There was that surfer again! He was wearing a black wet suit and was riding a high rolling wave for what seemed an interminable amount of time. She knew him by the glistening black hair, by his hawk-like style, and the fact that he steered clear of the surfers' beach, several hundred yards away.

"Well?"

Albertson's blue eyes fixed on Stacey. He smiled kindly.

"I don't know, Mr. Albertson. I'll have to think about this. And I want to discuss it with my folks."

"From a pure tennis point of view," said Lee Goodman, "it would be an excellent move. You'd get better coaching and more of it."

"You're pretty good," said Stacey.

"Up to a point," said Lee. "I guess I did a fine job with you, from eight to fifteen, but there are limitations to my skills. The hard fact is, Hank's a better coach, a tougher coach, and he knows more. Hey, I'm not proud. A fact's a fact."

Stacey had this sinking sensation she was losing a parent, that she was being shunted aside. Lee had been a kind of surrogate mother and buddy all in one low-keyed, good-humored package. Stacey had to remind herself this was the sort of move that happens when an athlete tries to improve herself. But the idea of playing on an all-boys' team was mind-boggling, especially with players like Keith and Van. She could not yet even begin to deal with the emotions that went with such a move.

"I never heard of a girl playing on a boys' team," said Stacey, finally. "Seems pretty intimate. Or am I being silly?"

"There was one case, ten years ago, in Louisiana," said Albertson. "Although it was on the college level, and the girl was already a nationally-ranked player. So you're right.

This would be the exception to the rule."

"Of course," said Stacey, more to herself, "there was a time when there were no women senators or representatives in Congress. And there was a time when a woman was never considered for the vice-presidency, much less the presidency."

"Girls have played with boys on little league baseball teams," said Lee.

"Yeah," said Stacey, "but this isn't little league."

"I'm aware of the social pressure," said Albertson. "But my main concern is tennis. You'd be an asset to the team. I watched you and Keith play doubles. I watched you against Van Larsen. You aced him. You returned his hard serve very easily."

Stacey stood up and stepped onto the sand. She turned her back to the ocean, to the lonely surfer who was paddling out into the rough waters. She thrust her hands into her jacket pockets and faced the two coaches. Stacey looked directly into Albertson's clear blue eyes.

"Think I could be number one?" she asked.

Her heart was pounding wildly. Her brain was slowly grappling with the reality of the moment. Here she was, Stacey King, being asked to play on a really terrific team. Here she was, a girl, being asked to compete with boys and against boys. Now a disturbing voice hissed in the back of her head, Hey, Stacey King, are you a girl? Or are you a tennis machine? Remember what Chuck

Jones said? Or was it Stan Jones? Or was it Sally Llewellyn? How does Keith Flowers see you? Does he see you at all?

"You can only improve a hundred percent," said Albertson. "You'll have terrific competition. Your practice sessions would be with Van and Keith and the Jones boys. When you compete against other schools, you'll be going up against some tough boys. . . ."

"What do you mean, 'when I compete' . . . ?"

"Just what I said," said Albertson. "You'll have to fight for your team ranking. There are no favorites. It's strictly based on performance — in practice matches and in school matches."

"Yeah," said Stacey, "I guess the important thing is that my game can only get better. I'm just worried about what people are going to say. It could really cause a stink."

"Are you kidding?" cried Lee. "This school — this town — doesn't even know that we have a tennis team. When did we ever have a big turnout?"

"When did we ever have a turnout?"

"Hardly anyone comes to watch the boys' team," said Albertson, "except maybe some girl friends of the players."

Stacey wanted to ask, Would that include Debby Klinger? The next moment, she tried to wipe the thought out of her mind. Keith was just another good-looking athlete, like Van Larsen . . . like that wet-suited surfer out there riding the waves. Time to get back to reality. Back to tennis!

"So what do you think?" asked Hank Albertson. "Ready to become a pioneer woman, breaking boundaries, setting new trails?"

Stacey's reply was immediate.

"No."

But with the next breath she said, "On the other hand, I'd get to play with Van . . . and Keith . . . and Stan."

"And, eventually," said coach Albertson, "you'd be competing against some top schools. You'd improve like crazy."

Like crazy, thought Stacey. Like crazy.

"I have to think it over," she announced. "And I've got to talk it over."

The beachfront meeting was over. Stacey put her canvas bag into the wire basket of her bike, threw the tennis bag over her shoulder, and rode away toward home.

Five

Stacey sat at the dinner table with her family and ate everything that was set before her. Lucinda King had prepared shrimp creole, just the way her Cajun mother had prepared it when they lived in the bayou country of central Louisiana. Stacey ate every shrimp, every bit of rice, ham, onion, and green pepper. She ate hot rolls and butter. She drank several glasses of cranberry juice. Michael talked about his upcoming concert in Tallahassee. Stacey continued to eat. Bill King talked about some new prescription drugs to relieve pain. Stacey ate more shrimp creole. For dessert, there was hot apple pie and peach ice cream. Lucinda talked about a new French movie that was playing in town. Stacey ate a second dessert.

"You want to come to the movies?" Mrs. King asked her daughter.

"No, Mom."

"Had enough to eat?" asked Mr. King, with a devilish wink in his eye.

"Yes, Dad."

"Good. Then you and your brother can clean up. Your mother and I are going to the movies."

Their parents were gone, and the aroma of creole hot sauce hovered over the dining room table.

Stacey still had not mentioned Albertson's offer. As Michael washed the pots and pans and Stacey dried them, she continued to maintain her silence. The whole notion suddenly seemed ridiculous. She wasn't a United States congresswoman. She wasn't a little-leaguer. She wasn't even a nationally-ranked tennis player going to a Louisiana college. She was just a fifteen-year-old kid playing for a small high-school team. Sure, she had a dream of playing big-time tennis. And she had a dream of dating some good-looking guys, but dreams were easy to live with. All of a sudden, here was a crazy reality intruding — Stacey playing on a boys' team. Nothing in her fifteen years had prepared her for this turn of events. It was all too much.

"Hey, Mikey, you want to take a drive to Runaway Beach?"

The King family had a small beach house eight miles north of Neptune. For Stacey, it was like a hideout where she could lose herself whenever Neptune threatened to close in on her. Armed with books and tapes, she would bike furiously up the service road that paralleled the parkway. Then she would sit on the ramshackle porch that fronted the empty beach, play her country music, read romantic novels, go for a long run along the shore, or just hang out and look at the birds, the sea, and the sky. Michael often went there alone to practice. Their parents went there on Sundays and on summer weekends.

"Sure," said Michael. "I can tell you've got big problems on your mind."

"What makes you think I've got problems?"

"The way you were gobbling down that food," said Michael. "I know you burn up a lot of energy playing tennis. I know you need a lot of protein. But tonight was ridiculous."

"You think tonight was ridiculous?" asked Stacey with a sardonic grin. "Today was unbelievable."

"Let's talk about it when we get the sea air in our faces," said Michael.

"Good," said Stacey. "Sea air gives me an appetite."

Stacey waited in the car while Michael made some "last-minute phone calls."

"Let's go in there," shouted Stacey. "Let's move it!"

She was feeling restless. Pam Hayward was going to a dance at Hermosa Pier. So was Julia and half the school. A new rock and roll band, MX Missile, was performing there for the first time. Sally and Van were going. Bridget was going. Stacey assumed that Keith and the dark-haired beauty were going. So why am I going to Runaway Beach with my brother? thought Stacey. Why do I have all these problems? I'll bet I'm the only girl in Neptune with problems, mused Stacey.

A half-hour later, she and Michael were sitting on the front porch in wicker rocking chairs, looking up at the Big Dipper. The cool breeze coming in off the ocean breathed new life into Stacey's body.

"Okay, Mikey, it's talking time. I've got a few things to sort out."

"I know all about it."

"What do you mean, you know all about it? Nobody knows, except. . . . "

"I know you want to be going out with guys," said Michael. "And I've been giving serious thought to your problem."

Stacey let out a big laugh.

"Serious thought? You sound like a shrink on TV."

"Listen," said Michael, "if you're going to make fun of. . . . "

"I'm sorry," said Stacey, and she meant it. "I've been on edge. In fact, I think I've been uptight for a while."

"Just hear me out, Stace. I know you've been uptight. I've got eyes. I know you'd like to be dating. You're fifteen years old. You don't want to be spending Friday night with your older brother, sitting around in an old beach house."

"I like hanging out with you," said Stacey,

smiling kindly at him. "Besides, it's not such an old beach house."

"Very funny," said Michael. "But I happen to know that you're not meeting the right guys."

"Mikey, that's not what I wanted to talk about."

"I know it's not easy for a fifteen-year-old girl to talk about her personal problems with her older brother...."

Stacey shook her head and relaxed. The discussion of joining the boys' tennis team might have to wait until the family sat down again at the dinner table. Just as well, thought Stacey. I have to figure out what I want. I have to weigh the pros and the cons. I have to consider whether or not I can take the razzing that's sure to come from people — and if it's going to be worth it. Stacey kept asking herself how much she was willing to put up with in order to be a truly first-class tennis player. Certainly, the opportunity was there.

Michael had not stopped talking.

". . . so I think we'll just take a ride over to Hermosa Pier. Hey, Stace, have you been listening?"

"Hermosa Pier. Sure. Take a ride."

"So let's go," said Michael.

"Huh? Where? Hermosa Pier? Right now? I'm not dressed!"

"Roberta's going to be there," said Michael. "She wants to catch this new group, MX something or other. No need to dress up. You look fine."

"Are you kidding?"

Stacey stood up. She was wearing old jeans, beat-up tennis shoes, and a navy blue sweatshirt with a hood. The front of the sweatshirt read, "Eat Fish" in small white letters.

"It's not going to be a fashion show or anything," said Michael. "Just getting together with some friends to hear some music."

"Hey wait a minute, King," said Stacey, pushing her brother back down into the rocking chair, "what's all this about 'some friends.' What's on your mind — besides a Beethoven violin concerto?"

Michael stood up quickly and jiggled the car keys.

" 'Some friends' means 'some friends.' I want to see Roberta. You want to meet . . . new people. We're all going to be standing around or dancing or something . . . in a big, dark place with some revolving lights and a lot of music."

"I'm no fool, King-O," said Stacey. "You've got some guy standing by, like a blind date. You think I want to meet some new guy when I'm wearing a sweatshirt that says 'Eat Fish?' "

"Stacey, Stacey, you're making too much out of this. Nobody's forcing you to go. Nobody's going to make you stay. You like

Roberta. She likes you. If you like my . . . other friends . . . that's okay. If you don't like them, that's also okay."

"You're so cool, Mister King," said Stacey, following him out to the car. She paused to kick the sand out of her sneakers while Michael started up the engine.

"Anyway," she shouted, "I don't have any money. You got the price of admission for both of us?"

"Of course I do," said Michael with a smug look on his face. "I think of everything."

Stacey tucked the sneakers under her arms as she hopped into the car. Seconds later, Michael made a screeching U-turn and was heading down the parkway toward Hermosa Pier.

"So tell me about this guy?" she asked.

"What guy?" asked Michael, innocently.

"Okay, then tell me about your 'friends.' "

Stacey turned the rear-view mirror toward her face and tried to fix her hair. She took a small brush from the pouch of her sweatshirt and began brushing vigorously.

"Could you put the top up?" she asked.

"Your hair looks fine," said Michael, re-adjusting the rear-view mirror.

Stacey slumped down in the seat. This was going to be a continuation of a very crazy day. Here she was, faced with a monumental problem, and her nice, quiet brother is taking her for a meeting with "friends." Her hair was kind of wild and her outfit was decidedly casual. Stacey found herself getting excited. Time for a change, she thought. What's the worst that can happen? It's not like I'm dating Keith Flowers.

Stacey imagined what it would be like, going on a date wth Keith or Van or anybody. She'd be preparing for hours. The end result would be that she'd look like she was getting ready for the finals of a tennis match. Same hairdo, probably the same outfit, probably the same attitude.

Stacey put her bare feet on the dashboard and combed her hair with her fingers.

"Okay, Michael, let's move this crate! Hermosa Pier, and step on it. I want to hear this hot new group, see what all the fuss is about. So move it!"

"Yes, boss," said her brother, smiling broadly.

"Hermosa" in Spanish means beautiful, lovely. There was nothing particularly beautiful or lovely about the cavernous auditorium built out over the green waters of Pelican Beach. The structure was built fifty-one years ago as nothing more than a covered space to attract big bands and marathon dancers. The colored revolving lights were the only concession to current style. The big bands had been replaced by quartets, quintets, and sextets of scruffy musicians with high-powered amplifiers and enough electrical energy to shake up the sea life for miles around. Young dancers still had the energy to dance all night, if not all weekend, like the two-stepping couples from their grand-parents' generation.

The dance hall at Hermosa Pier was high, wide, and noisy. As long as it was crowded, you didn't pay much attention to its sleazi-ness. After midnight, however, it threatened to turn back into a poor old pumpkin of a seedy amusement pier.

Stacey and Michael walked through the mirrored lobby filled with Neptune High students. Stacey checked out the various out-fits, which ranged from sloppy to sporty to dressy. She waved to some classmates as her brother purchased the tickets.

And there was Pam Hayward coming to-ward her with a very tall, good-looking boy named Dave Kelly. He was the star center of the basketball team.

"Hey, Stacey, what are you doing here?" shouted Pam.

"Same thing you're doing here," Stacey shouted back.

"Got a date?" asked Pam.

"Maybe," said Stacey.

"Maybe?"

Stacey pretended an aloofness that hid her excitement.

"I have to check him out," she said.

"What's his name?" asked Pam.

Stacey tugged at Michael's sleeve.

"What's my date's name?" she asked.

"Who said you had a date," said Michael, feigning innocence. Stacey turned to Pam.

"He doesn't have a name," said Stacey.

Dave Kelly gestured to Pam to hurry up.

"My All-American center seems to be impatient," whispered Pam. "I think he's dance-mad. You know these jocks. They're really dancing fiends," said Pam as Dave pulled her into the dance hall.

The next moment, Stacey and Michael entered a world of rainbow lights flashing on and off, dazzling and blinding a sea of bobbing, gyrating bodies. MX Missile had not yet made its appearance. Meanwhile, the enormous space was vibrating with the sounds of British rock, Jamaican reggae, and new wave punk bands. The disc jockey kept mixing the styles, blending skillfully from one to another. The crowd loved it.

Stacey followed Michael to a bar at the far end of the hall. Her eyes were still not accustomed to the darkness and the bursts of colored lights. The music was loud and she loved it. Suddenly there was Roberta Bell, reaching out for Michael's outstretched hand. Roberta was two inches shorter than Stacey, freckle-faced, and strawberry-blond. Her big glasses could not hide her lively, light blue eyes. She was pretty and fun and Michael was crazy about her.

"Hi, Stacey," screamed Roberta, trying to be heard above the din.

"Hey, Roberta," Stacey screamed back. "Didn't recognize you without your cello!"

"Didn't recognize you without your tennis racquets. Glad you could make it. It's a nice surprise."

"For me, too," said Stacey.

The next thing Stacey knew, a big, muscular young man in a tight-fitting tennis shirt was standing alongside her. Michael had his arm around the guy's well-developed shoulder.

"Stacey, this is my friend, Wally Baxter."

Stacey looked up to an attractive, serious-faced young man with short, curly brown hair.

"Hi, Stacey," said Wally in a deep, growly voice.

"Hi."

Stacey thought of saying something corny like, "Do you come here often?" but she simply smiled quickly. Then she half-opened her mouth to say, "Quite a turnout," but rejected those words as being too obvious, and then she simply shut up. Wally had no problem with Stacey's shyness. He began talking loudly about himself, about the Neptune football team (he was the star linebacker), about his future plans (he had a football scholarship to the University of Miami), and about MX Missile (they weren't nearly as good as Trash or Mother's Helpers).

"Anything you want to know," shouted Michael, his arms around Roberta and Wally, "just ask Mister Muscles over here."

Stacey noted that Wally enjoyed that nickname. Before she could take a deep breath and mutter something about the weather, a loud metallic voice blared, "And now, ladies and gentlemen, direct from their sensational appearance at Tarpon Springs, here's . . . MX Missile!"

Four very thin young men with their heads cleanly shaven, except for jagged strips down the center of their skulls like Indian feathers, shuffled onto the stage. The audience shrieked, stamped their feet, and clapped their hands wildly.

"Last place I expected to be," said Stacey with genuine excitement.

"Why?" asked Wally.

Stacey shrugged her shoulders. The band started playing and singing. Soon there were couples filling every empty space on the floor, dancing, swaying, bobbing like corks on the ocean.

"Want to dance?" asked Wally.

"Me?"

Stacey felt her legs nailed to the wooden floor.

"I don't mean your brother," joked Wally.

He took her hand and guided Stacey to the center of the pulsating hall. Stacey's fingers were enveloped by his thick paw. The sea of dancers parted miraculously as Wally cleared a path. Wally hunched his shoulders and began to dance. Stacey just stood there and watched him. After a full minute, Wally asked, "What's the matter?"

"I have to get into it," explained Stacey.

"Just follow me," he instructed her. "I'll get you into it."

Stacey began to dance. Or, more precisely, she moved her left leg, then her right leg, then the left again, then the right again. Wally's eyes were closed. MX Missile had lifted him up and out of Hermosa Pier. He was gone. Stacey relaxed and grinned.

Okay, she thought, I can follow that.

She was about to close her eyes when Keith Flowers danced into view. His light hair was glistening with perspiration. At first it appeared that he was alone. Then a curvaceous, frizzy-haired girl slithered into view. She put her ringed fingers around Keith's waist. He never missed a beat, nor did she. Stacey recognized her as Jackie Girard, a junior with the reputation as the sexiest dancer at Neptune High. She was also president of the Student Council. Stacey's feet suddenly became leaden. She wanted to turn her sweatshirt inside out, to hide the "Eat Fish" emblazoned across her chest.

"You're doing fine," shouted Wally, whose eyes opened briefly, then closed.

"Yeah," said Stacey. "It just takes me a while."

"What?" asked Wally.

"Music makes me smile," she mumbled.

"Yeah, they're not bad," said Wally, closing his eyes again and raising his arms above his head to reveal his biceps.

Stacey felt a tapping on her shoulder. She turned around. There was Keith, half-smiling down at her.

"Having a good time?" he asked, with a twinkle in his eye.

"I like the band," she answered honestly.

Keith began dancing in place with Stacey. Jackie Girard was doing a major solo number directly behind him.

"She's good," said Stacey, pointing over Keith's shoulder.

"She's great," cried Keith.

For the next twenty minutes, Stacey danced in her little space. Sometimes she danced with Wally. Sometimes she danced with Keith. Mostly she just moved slowly in place, enjoying the music and vaguely wondering what these two boys were all about.

Stacey couldn't tell if Wally was involved with the blaring, funky music or with himself. He certainly wasn't holding back with his dancing. Wally appeared to be enjoying his own body. Keith had turned away and was frankly admiring the expert, almost balletic movement of Jackie Girard. She was good! Stacey noticed that Keith did not make a big deal out of being with Jackie. He didn't act possessive or anything. He was just having fun dancing with her. A parade of friends and acquaintances began to appear. Pam waved to her and yelled something as she slid past with Dave Kelly. Sally and Van Larsen boogied by her, stopped, and included her in a fast-paced movement. And there was Bobbie Rose with her date; Julia De Diego was with a funny-looking kid she'd never seen before; Bridget Salmon and Chuck Jones — or was it Stan Jones? — were there together. A crazy thought popped into Stacey's head. What if she ran up to the band-

stand and announced that she was invited
to join the boys' tennis team. Stacey giggled
nervously at the notion. Would she be greeted
by applause? Cat-calls and hisses? Silence?

"What's the matter? Aren't you dancing?"

Michael was beside her now, holding
Roberta's hand. He was staring at his sister
with genuine concern.

"I'm tired," said Stacey. "I mean, I'm
really beat. It's been a long, long day."

"Tell your date to take you home," ad-
vised Roberta.

"My date?" asked Stacey.

"The incredible hulk," said Roberta, pointing to the hard-dancing Wally. "He can dance
all night. In fact, he probably will dance all
night if you don't drag him off the floor."

Wally drove Stacey home. They sat in the
car for a while as he talked about MX Missile, giving a detailed criticism of the group.
Stacey was impressed by his musical knowledge. He also talked about Neptune sports,
including tennis. Again, she found herself
listening with interest. The guy knew what
he was talking about.

"Want to go to a movie next week, like
next Saturday night?" he asked. "There's an
old Japanese movie, *Rashomon*, playing at
the Dungeon. It's a classic. I've seen it twice
already."

"Okay."

Wally hopped out of the car, quickly
walked to the other side and opened Stacey's
door.

A perfect gentleman, she thought.

"I'll pick you up at seven," said Wally. "Don't be late. I can't stand coming in on the middle of a picture."

"I know," said Stacey. "I'm the same way."

That was that. Wally got back into the car and drove off.

"Oh yeah," said Stacey to the departing car. "Thanks for a lovely evening."

She laughed at herself and shook her head. She tiptoed into the house. It was only when Stacey had finished washing her face and brushing her teeth that it occurred to her that something had been wrong. Nothing serious, she figured, but there was something odd about Wally Baxter. Oh, well, she reasoned, he seems harmless enough and interesting enough . . . and it's about time I started dating. But Wally, like Keith, like joining the boys' tennis team, was still a question mark.

S^{ix}

Stacey woke up early on Saturday morning to the squawking of seagulls.

"Oh nuts," she mumbled as she rolled out of bed, "somebody must be dumping garbage into the canal. No civic pride in Neptune."

Moments later, the cries of the scavenger birds were gone, replaced by the sweet violin sounds of Michael practicing in his room. Stacey smiled as she rummaged through the cedar chest, looking for clean tennis clothes. She yawned loudly as she slipped into white tennis shorts, white cotton socks, and scruffy sneakers. Then she stumbled into the bathroom, brushed her teeth, and vigorously washed her face. The events of the previous day and night rushed through her awakening head. She found a red, white, and blue striped tennis shirt and somehow managed to get her flailing head and arms through all the right openings. Stacey looked at herself in the full-length closet mirror.

"Stacey King," she announced, "new star of the Neptune High . . . boys' tennis team. Oh wow!"

She grabbed a new can of tennis balls, threw them into her racquet bag, and headed for the kitchen. The violin playing had stopped. Her family was seated around the kitchen table. Michael was munching on a big grapefruit and studying a sheet of music. Even with a mouthful of grapefruit wedges, he was managing to hum a few bars of a Beethoven piece. Bill King was reading the front page of the Neptune News and sipping coffee. Lucinda King was reading the back page, held aloft by her husband like a table divider. She, too, was sipping coffee. Stacey took in the domestic scene, then reached for the bran flakes, a banana, and milk. This was her standard breakfast, along with either a fresh grapefruit or orange.

"Morning, everyone," said Stacey.

"How was your date?" asked Mrs. King.

"Okay."

"How about a word of thanks," said Michael, "from the guy who brought you two together?"

Stacey brought the bowl of cereal to the table and sat down. A spoon, she thought. That's what was missing — a spoon.

"It's not like Wally and I are getting married. It was just one sneaky blind date. But thanks."

"I only want my kid sister to be happy," said Michael.

Stacey took a deep breath as she looked from her father to her brother to her mother. She loved them all very much. They were certainly all strong individuals. They argued and they fought. They ignored one another (as they were doing now at the breakfast table).

Stacey respected each of them for, among other things, the support system they provided her. But they never hesitated to criticize, to speak their opinions openly in what was usually a constructive fashion. In a few seconds, she would put them all to the test.

"Hey, everybody," she shouted, "family discussion time!" Bill King peered at her from over his coffee cup.

"Morning, Stacey," he said.

"Morning, Dad."

Lucinda King took hold of the newspaper with both hands and yanked it away. She folded it neatly across her lap as Michael looked up and laughed.

"If you're going to discuss your heavy date with Wally," said Michael, "count me out."

"No, Mikey Mouse," said Stacey, "I'm not discussing my new social life. I have more important things to talk about."

Her parents put down their coffee cups. Their concentration was fully on their daughter.

"You know Hank Albertson," began Stacey. "He's the coach of the Neptune boys' team. Well, it seems that he's been scouting me for the past month or so. And he's been having heavy discussions with Lee. Anyway. . . ."

Stacey paused to shovel a spoonful of banana, milk, and bran-flakes into her mouth.

"Don't talk with a full mouth," her mother said. "We'll wait."

"Anyway," said Stacey, gulping down her breakfast, "Coach Albertson wants me on the . . . boys' team."

Bill King took a long swallow of his coffee. Lucinda King studied her daughter's eyes. Michael reached for a fresh banana.

"Don't everyone speak at once," said Stacey.

"Where will you take your showers?" asked Michael, grinning broadly.

"Where I always take my showers," snapped Stacey. "Come on, be serious."

Bill King tapped his fingers and rubbed the corners of his mouth. There was a hard expression on his face.

"I think it's a fantastic opportunity," he said, finally. "Except for your tournaments, which aren't very often, you've got almost no competition. Now you can play all the top juniors. It's going to do wonders for your game."

"Even though most guys will be stronger than me?" argued Stacey. "Even though I'll probably get beaten all the time . . . if I'm lucky enough to play!"

"But this is exactly the time to make a move," said her father. "Sure, it's better to win than to lose. But you have to lose before you can win. Being the best without having to try can bring down the level of your game.

"You're on your way to becoming a superior athlete," her father continued. "It will give you more of a challenge than Sally or Bobbie Rose."

"Pam has a good serve," said Stacey, feeling very unsure about everything. "And I've got to meet her in a few minutes." She gulped down a tall glass of milk.

"You're going to be the joke of Neptune," said Lucinda King.

She stood up suddenly and walked to the window, pushing it open and breathing in the fresh morning air. Lucinda King was a delicate woman — thin lips, narrow nose, fine features. Along with a lyrical Louisiana accent, her manner was totally deceptive. Mrs. King was the brains of the King Pharmacy and the rock of the family. When she was Stacey's age, she had dreams of going to college and becoming a doctor. Coming from a dirt poor family, she believed that her entry to a good state school would be through her tennis skills, if not her considerable academic achievements. Unfortuntely, it was during the time of the Great Depression. Mrs. King had to give up the luxury of tennis and college. Her father argued that girls weren't accepted into medical school anyway, so why waste the time. Lucinda did not believe in wasting time. She worked as a waitress by day and studied pharmacology at night. Somehow, she never picked up a tennis racquet competitively again. But she made sure that her daughter would have it all: the tennis, the education, everything!

"Child, they're going to laugh you off the court and out of school!" said Lucinda. "You'll be considered a freak."

"My daughter is not going to be considered. . . ." began Bill King.

"Dad, I can speak for myself," said Stacey. "Mom, nobody at Neptune cares about tennis. Nobody comes to the girls' matches or the boys' matches. Hardly anyone plays the game. The one reason coach Albertson wants me is because he sees my potential."

"Well," said Lucinda, "any fool can see your potential. And you'll realize your potential when you play your holiday and your summer tournaments."

"That'll take too long," argued Stacey. "I play the Easter Bowl and about five summer tournaments. That's not enough. That's why I'm not 'match tough.'"

Lucinda nodded. But she remained tight-lipped.

"I'm all for Stacey joining the boys' team," said Michael. "Only now it'll have to be retitled 'the persons' team.' Besides, if girls and guys can play mixed doubles, why can't they play mixed singles? My vote's for Stacey accepting the offer."

"Stacey," said her mother, "if you can put up with people making fun of you, pointing their fingers at you, not talking to you, then go ahead and do it."

"I don't care what people might say," said Stacey, knowing that wasn't exactly true. She thought of the "tennis machine" label that had been slapped on her. She bristled at the image and wondered if Keith Flowers thought of her that way.

"Well," said Stacey, "I've got to go and meet Pam. Thanks for your advice. I mean that."

"What about your advice?" asked her father. "What do you want?"

"I'm thinking of what mom said. I don't know if I can take the kids at school making fun of me. Maybe they won't, but I don't know if I want to take that chance."

Bill King looked at his wife.

"There aren't all that many chances in life," he said. "Sometimes you have to take the chances you can get."

Lucinda studied her husband's face.

Stacey opened the front door and squinted into the warm morning sun.

"I hear you, Dad," she said, putting one foot outside onto the rubber mat.

"And sometimes," cried Lucinda King, "you have to make your own chances. It's your decision, honey."

Stacey nodded thoughtfully. She blew kisses to her family, then turned and started to run toward the school courts. She was already fifteen minutes late, which was very unusual for Stacey King.

The school courts were surprisingly crowded on this balmy Saturday morning. What's happening? wondered Stacey. Has Neptune suddenly discovered racquet sports?

Pam Hayward was sitting on the court, cross-legged, with her back to the net. She was strumming her racquet like a guitar.

"Hey, Stace, don't hurry on my account. What happened? Wally keep you out too late?"

Stacey looked past her friend to the adjoining court. Sally and Van Larsen were playing doubles against Bobbie Rose . . . and Keith Flowers. Without even thinking, Stacey untied her beige bandanna, vigorously combed her hair, then retied it.

"You don't have to fuss for me," Pam said with a grin. When she saw Stacey watching Keith so attentively, she asked, "Have you dumped Wally already? Girl, you sure move fast!"

Stacey opened a fresh can of balls, pausing to enjoy the hissing sound as the air escaped from the cylinder. She smiled sardonically at Pam, then bounced each of the new balls carefully.

"Hey, Hayward, I'm onto your sarcasm. I'm not dumping anybody. I just want to play tennis. Here, have a ball. Have two."

Pam rose slowly but made no effort to go over or around the net. Nor did Stacey move back to the baseline. Her eyes were fixed on the mixed doubles game. She imagined strolling over and announcing her decision to play on the boys' team. Would Van make one of his wise-guy cracks? Would Keith look on her as a female super-jock? Would Sally . . . ? But Stacey could not speculate. She realized how little she knew of her schoolmates.

"You okay, Stace?" asked Pam.

"Oh yeah, sure. I just want to do some stretching exercises."

She placed her racquet on the ground, then began turning her shoulders from side to side. This was followed by a dance exercise, raising her right arm over her head, the fingers extended toward her left ear. After a few easy stretches, she raised her left arm over her head with the fingers extended to her right ear.

Now she noticed someone moving just outside the adjoining court, taking pictures of Keith! The camera hid the photographer's face. But there was no mistaking the dark hair and the long legs — it was Debby Klinger.

"Boy, that Keith Flowers really gets around," mused Stacey. "Last night it was Jackie Girard. This morning it's Debby. No wonder he looks tired all the time."

"I think they're just friends," said Pam. "Seriously. He's a nice guy. Girls naturally gravitate toward him."

"I don't," lied Stacey, wondering why she said that.

"I didn't say, every girl. No need to get defensive, Ms. King."

"I thought we were playing tennis, Ms. Hayward."

"I don't see any balls going over the net," said Pam. "And I don't see any racquets being swung."

Stacey looked at her friend for a full thirty seconds.

"Pam," Stacey said seriously, "I need to talk to you."

Stacey told Pam the story of Hank Albertson's invitation. Pam listened attentively, then let out a low whistle.

"What's your gut reaction?" she asked finally.

"To go for it," answered Stacey immediately, gulping hard.

"Okay then," said Pam. "Listen to yourself. And go for it."

Stacey pointed to the four players on the adjoining court. At that precise moment, Van walked toward them.

"You girls come here to talk or to play?" he shouted with a wide grin. "I want to see some action over there!"

Stacey took a deep breath, then walked toward Van and the others. She was clutching the racquet in her right hand. Sally, Bobbie Rose, and Keith were now catching the scene. They stood motionless on the court. There was an eerie silence in the air.

"Hi, everybody," said Stacey with a forced nonchalance. "Nice day."

Van chuckled.

"This weather report was brought to you by Stacey King. Thank you, Stacey."

"What's up?" asked Sally.

Stacey told the group about Albertson's offer to join the boys' team. Even as the words were pouring out, she kept hearing Pam's words, "Listen to yourself. And go for it." That had always been Stacey's philosophy. Why was she now so hesitant? Why did she need everyone's approval? Stacey did not have the answers to these questions.

Keith was the first to step forward. He held out his hand and said, "Welcome to the team."

"I haven't said anything to coach Albertson," said Stacey, feeling Keith's genuine warmth. "I want to let him know this week. So, all of you please don't spread this around until I speak to him."

"It's not like we're going to call a press conference for the TV reporters," snickered Van. "But I think it's great. Congratulations. Anyway, we need some pretty faces on the team."

Sally and Bobbie Rose looked at one another. The usually bubbly Bobbie Rose appeared subdued. "I thought that girls played on the girls' team and boys played on the boys' team," she said. "Isn't that what it's all about?"

"I don't know," answered Stacey. "I think it's just about playing tennis the best way you can."

Pam Hayward was alongside her, suggesting they go back to their court.

"Come on, Stace, let's play before we lose the court."

Sally Llewellyn had still not said anything. Finally she spoke. "I don't know that you're going to help the boys' team, but you sure are going to hurt our team. If you go, there's no way we're going to win anything."

"You never win anyway," said Van. "Stacey's the only one who comes out on top."

"That's a mean thing to say," cried Sally.

"Hey, come on," said Stacey. "I didn't want to start a fight. I'm just letting you know what's happening and that I'm thinking about it. If I go ahead with it, I don't want the news to come as a complete surprise."

Stacey and Pam walked back to their court and started to warm up. Debby Klinger continued to take pictures from the sidelines. The camera seemed to be permanently joined to her face. She peered through the lens and focused on Keith's serene face, fully concentrated as he prepared to receive service. A snap of the shutter and she swerved her camera to find Sally, across the net, tight-lipped and distracted. Debby did not take the picture.

It was a tense week for Stacey. She had her family's tacit support; now the decision was up to her. She attended classes and wondered what Julia, Bridget, and the others would think. She practiced every afternoon and silently questioned every move and expression from the team. Lee Goodman was already preparing for Stacey's decision. The coach had invited two ninth-graders, Carrie Edison and Shirl Walker, to participate in the practice sessions. The newcomers looked good to Stacey and that was a relief. It would make the transition easier.

Saturday came before she knew it, and Wally was at the front door. She could hear his loud, excited voice talking to Michael while she adjusted her blue blouse and white jeans. Stacey scrutinized her image in the mirror.

"So this is the pretty face that's joining the boys' team," she muttered. "What can go wrong?"

She had no answers as she hurried out the door, greeted Wally with a nervous smile, waved goodbye to her brother, and walked out the door.

For the next two hours, Stacey never got to open her mouth. Wally talked on and on about football practice, his significant contribution to the team, the pending football scholarship, the upcoming season, and his healthful diet.

"Liquids," he confided in her. "That's the key to physical and mental health. Lots of liquids. Fresh fruit juices, fresh vegetable juices, and milk. Absolutely clears the stomach. Does wonders for the brain. And feel these biceps. Hard as a rock!"

Wally hunched over the wheel of the car. Stacey glanced at his bulging arms.

"Uh-huh," she said. "Yeah. They look, um, muscular."

Wally did stop talking when the movie began. Although the film was in Japanese, Stacey had no problems with the English subtitles. She enjoyed the story which was about how various Japanese travelers experienced one intensely dramatic event and later had totally different versions of what had actually occurred. Two hours later Stacey was following Wally back out to the parking lot. She was eager to discuss the movie.

"That was one wild movie," exclaimed Stacey. "Makes you wonder whether two people can ever agree on anything!"

"The movie is about the nature of truth," Wally declared solemnly, looking over Stacey's head to the line of people shuffling into the nine o'clock show. He waved to some friends. "It's also about how truth is perceived," Wally continued.

"Yeah," agreed Stacey. "I'm on the verge of making a big move. I wonder how people will perceive what I'm doing and why I'm doing it."

She paused, feeling good about her ability to express her thoughts with Wally. Stacey had to remind herself that this was only her first real date with an upperclassman. It was easy. She asked herself what all the fuss and worry had been about? So she was a late bloomer! Wally didn't exactly get to her like

Keith Flowers did. But Stacey had time. There would be lots of dates — with lots of boys. Pam always cautioned her, "Take it one date at a time. You never know about a guy, first time out."

Wally opened the car door for her, then ran around the front as Stacey reached over and pushed open the door for him. He picked some loose threads off his tight-fitting, V-necked, white cotton sweater.

"Oh yeah," said Stacey, a little too loudly, "I'm about to make a real big move!"

She figured that he would be intrigued by her provocative statement. Wally put the key in the ignition and started the car.

"Big doings at Hermosa Pier," he said. "One of my favorite groups, Trash, is back in town. Now you'll hear some *real* music."

"I like to hear real music," said Stacey, a bit deflated. "Oh, and thanks for the movie. It was a treat."

"My pleasure," said Wally magnanimously, as he zoomed out of the parking lot.

It was a pleasantly warm evening with a sky full of stars as Wally drove and talked, along Pelican Parkway. Stacey relaxed and let the breeze caress her face. Suddenly there was a tie-up as they got within a mile of the Pier. Wally began to rage and fume at the stalled traffic.

"I'm looking forward to seeing your group," said Stacey, trying to soothe him by changing the subject. "Thanks for taking me."

Wally seemed taken aback by this expression of gratitude.

"It's not *my* group," he began, ". . . but thanks. I mean, that's okay. I like to dance."

"Looks like the cars are beginning to move," said Stacey. "I guess everybody's going to see Trash."

The cars inched forward. Wally was unusually quiet. Stacey figured that since he apparently wasn't able to ask even the simplest questions, she would take the initiative and volunteer her big news. Wally listened to the story of Hank Albertson and Stacey's mixed feelings about joining the boys' team. Fifteen minutes later, he pulled into the parking lot at Hermosa Pier.

"You have to look at the big picture," said Wally.

For a second or so, Stacey thought he was talking about another movie. Wally combed his hair, got out quickly, and began talking. Stacey simply slid across and let herself out of the car. The Pier was crowded with kids from the school. They were arriving in groups of two's and three's and more. There were lots of unfamiliar faces. Wally was talking loudly as he grabbed Stacey's hand and led her through the crowd, like a downfield blocker in a football game.

"I mean," continued Wally, "you have to consider the overall picture. You probably think this is going to be a step up the ladder."

She ran to keep abreast of him. He gave two tickets to a dour young man in a white suit, then motioned Stacey to fall in behind him. There was already a long line in the lobby.

"Yeah sure," said Stacey, somewhat flustered as she squeezed in alongside him, "I was kind of proud to be asked."

"It'll be bad for your morale," he whispered. "Every guy that you play is going to have to beat you badly or else he'll lose face."

Stacey stretched her back and smiled.

"I'm not going to be playing any Japanese Samurai swordsman," she said. "It's not like they're going to commit hari kari if I win the match."

Wally put his right hand on Stacey's left shoulder. He shook his head slowly as if he was dealing with a five-year-old.

"You don't know the first thing about men," he confided in her, "especially American athletes. We're very proud."

Stacey considered these remarks.

"I think American women athletes have a lot of pride, too," she said.

But Wally continued to shake his head, more vigorously now. The long line of Trash fans was starting to move forward into the hall.

"So the more you get beaten, and you will get beaten," said Wally, "the worse you're going to feel about yourself."

The couple in front of them half-turned around to see who the potential loser was — Stacey hunched her shoulders and examined her white tennis shoes.

"Not only that," continued Wally, "everyone at school is going to point a finger at you as the Neptune weirdo."

Now the couple in front of them, two well-dressed youngsters in matching beige jumpsuits, did a three-quarter turn and openly stared at Stacey. Stacey stared back and crossed her eyes. The couple hastily turned back around.

"Hey, Wally," whispered Stacey, "it's only a game."

"To you, maybe. Not to the others."

The line moved swiftly forward. Stacey realized they were among the first to arrive. The great hall looked like a half-empty barn. She followed Wally to the mirrored bar.

"Like a soft drink?" he asked.

"Any fruit juices?"

Stacey couldn't resist adding, "I'm into liquids."

Wally had forgotten his own statement. He beamed at her, then ordered two pineapple juices. Stacey looked around. She didn't know anyone there. But the night was young, she thought. A disc jockey was playing tapes of MX Missile. Stacey was already feeling bored and restless.

"I'll tell you something," shouted Wally.

Stacey almost dropped her glass of juice. A few drops splattered on her white jeans. She grimaced, then licked her index finger and gently rubbed the spot.

"You're going to be treated like one of the boys," added Wally in an accusatory tone.

"It's not a normal way for a healthy teenager to grow up."

Wally spoke with such sincerity and concern that Stacey felt guilty for even considering the move. She thought about his words as they finished their drinks and watched the crowd. Not too many people were out on the floor. Instead, they were milling about, talking, craning their necks as they looked for friends, or just standing around waiting for Trash. Stacey felt unsettled. She was considering her date's words. After all, she thought, he must know what he's talking about, Wally is older, he's been around. Stacey had led a cloistered life, given over almost completely to the world of tennis matches and training. What did she know, Stacey asked herself, about the real worlds of dating and public opinion?

Sally and Van popped up from out of nowhere. They were both in a friendly, sympathetic mood as they greeted Stacey and Wally.

"Hey, Stacey," said Van, "get that worried look off your face. It's Saturday night."

"Well," said Stacey, "I'm still worried about you-know-what."

"Hey, kid," Van said, "you're making too much of it. I don't think it matters one way or another. Do what you want to do."

"Sure it matters," argued Sally. "Everybody's going to be down on Stacey. Girls on the track team are going to want to join the boys' track team. The girl gymnasts will want to mix with the boy gymnasts. It'll be crazy!"

Wally turned away from his crowd-watching and addressed the small circle.

"That's what I've been telling Stacey. There's going to be a lot of adverse public opinion. It's not worth it."

Stacey felt like she was suffocating. Then she spotted Keith Flowers. He was out on the floor, dancing with Jackie Girard. Their dancing was a contrast in styles and attitudes. Jackie, with her sinewy body and ballet dancer's legs, was putting on a great show, not only for Keith but for the Jones brothers. Chuck and Stan were standing off to the side, hypnotized by Jackie's sensual movements. Keith was barely moving, but he appeared to be totally involved with the hard-driving, syncopated rhythms.

"Wally," said Stacey, "let's go over there. I want to say hello to Keith. . . ."

"Yeah," he growled. "Your future teammate."

"Mine, too, maybe," Van shouted, as he took Sally's hand and danced her away. "Could be my new doubles partner!"

Wally trailed behind Stacey as they approached Keith and Jackie. Just then, the music stopped. There was a strange, sudden emptiness, as if all the air had been sucked out of the hall. Stacey felt a shock of self-consciousness as Keith called her name, smiled, and waved.

Jackie Girard quickly checked out Stacey, taking in her hair, blouse, pants, and shoes in one expert glance. Then she dismissed Stacey with a click of her chewing gum. Stan and Chuck Jones had been watching Jackie dance. They were an appreciative audience, as was Wally Baxter, who positioned himself between the Jones brothers.

"Hey, Jackie," Chuck shouted, "You dance really smooth."

"Yeah," chimed in Stan, "and you look great tonight. No kidding!"

Wally grunted approvingly as Jackie swung her hips and snapped her fingers. The sexy girl now addressed her male audience.

"You know, guys," said Jackie, "it's really important for a girl's date to be attractive. I mean, good-looking. Appearance is everything. 'Cause everything follows from that. Look good. Feel good. You have to look good and look right — the girl and the boy — together and separately."

The Jones boys nodded in unison. Each of them wanted to date Jackie Girard. Wally stood up straight, his massive arms folded across his chest, staring blankly at her. Stacey just stood there in disbelief, taking in the entire scene. This, she thought, is the kind of girl that Keith is interested in? She makes Debby Klinger look like a heavy thinker!

The disc jockey put on some new-wave rock and roll. Wally immediately moved forward and began dancing with Jackie.

"Fine with me," said Stacey to no one in particular. "Be my guest."

Keith had no visible reaction. He said something but Stacey couldn't hear him for the abrupt, loud music.

"Let's go outside," Keith shouted, as his hand softly grazed Stacey's shoulder.

Stacey nodded. She was glad to be getting away from the loud music and the crowd. She also looked forward to being alone with Keith. They passed a mirrored wall. Stacey sneaked a glance at herself. Now that the braids were gone, she liked the soft, natural flow of her hair, and the scooped-neck, blue blouse wasn't half-bad. Thanks to Pam, she was getting to be a cool dresser.

Keith and Stacey sat on the edge of the pier, watching the clouds drift past the half-moon. The sound of the surf mingled with the now-faint music. For a time, neither spoke.

"Thinking about the big problem?" asked Keith, finally.

"Yep."

She wasn't. She was just enjoying the presence of Keith Flowers. His words jarred her into reality.

"Think of yourself," he said. "In this situation, nobody else is important. Hey! Everybody's telling you what to do. But they're all speaking for themselves. They're really telling you what *they* would do. No one's in your shoes except you. And no one counts — except you."

"That sounds pretty selfish," Stacey suggested.

"Selfish doesn't have to be a dirty word," said Keith. "Besides, you're the one who's going to have to pay the price for any move you make, one way or another. The rest of us are going to go on with our lives. You're the one who's moving. I think you're moving *up*. Some people are jealous of you. Yeah, and some people are just plain negative about life. They'll say no to everything."

Stacey listened carefully. She wanted to know more about this enigmatic young man who was such a gifted athlete, so popular, and yet never traded on his popularity or good looks. He moved easily in and out of groups, always going his own way. At least, that was Stacey's perception of him.

And she knew, deep down, that Keith was right — just as Pam was right in encouraging her to "go for it." Stacey also knew that she was scared.

"You know," she said, breaking the silence, "this is the first time I'm actually having a social life. Like, I'm dating . . . different guys — well, I've dated two — and I'm starting to socialize with Sally's crowd. . . . "

"So you think this 'big move' could set you back socially?" asked Keith, who already knew the answer.

"Well, I want people to like me," confessed Stacey. "But I also want to be the best tennis player I can be. And Coach Albertson's giving me the opportunity. Do you think I'm beating this problem to death?"

They laughed loudly, mostly with relief.

"Yes, I do," said Keith. "Definitely."

"And I agree with me . . . and you, definitely," said Stacey.

At that exact moment, Wally came out onto the pier. He looked at the two of them, their legs dangling over the pier, and began shouting.

"I turn my back for one minute and you go running off with another guy."

"Easy, man," said Keith, "you're scaring away the gulls."

"I thought," said Stacey, "you were having a good time, dancing with Jackie."

A sheepish expression came over Wally's face.

"Sorry," he mumbled. "Okay. I'll see you inside."

"I'll be there in *one* minute," said Stacey.

"Trash is going on soon," explained Wally. He inadvertently flexed his biceps and his pectorals as he returned to the dance hall.

"I do believe that boy's crazy in love," said Keith.

"I do believe that boy's just plain crazy," said Stacey.

Keith stood up. He held out his hand. Stacey took it, feeling his gentleness and strength. Then he guided Stacey to her feet as she raised herself, their hands clasped tightly together.

"That was a good team effort," Keith said softly.

Stacey remained silent. She hurried back inside to rejoin her date.

Seven

Monday was an intense practice session for the girls' team. Lee Goodman shouted at everybody, including Stacey, that they were only playing "at fifty percent." The coach, with her gold-braided baseball cap pulled down low over her forehead, made everyone stay an extra hour to work on their serve-and-volley games. Even the two ninth-grade newcomers, Carrie Edison and Shirl Walker, were put through the rigors of the nonstop drills.

"Okay, Sally, you hit with Stacey on the number one court," barked the coach.

Goodman clapped her hands rapidly, indicating that the players were dragging their feet.

"I wonder what kind of a weekend Coach Goodman had," whispered Pam to Stacey as they switched courts. "She is one angry lady."

Stacey didn't say anything. But she assumed that the usually mild-mannered coach was upset because her number one player was on the verge of leaving. True, Lee Goodman had encouraged the move, if there was to be one. Perhaps, thought Stacey as she walked slowly onto the enclosed court, the woman realizes the difficult task of rebuilding a team. Maybe I should have more team spirit? More loyalty to my old coach and my teammates?

"You ready?" shouted Sally from across the net.

"Oh yeah, sure," Stacey shouted back. "Serve 'em up!"

Sally let loose with a spin serve to Stacey's backhand. As the tough, wiry Sally rushed toward the net, Stacey threw up a soft blooper. Without bothering to move back toward the center of the court, she watched as Sally easily put the ball away.

Stacey played in a distracted fashion for the next fifteen minutes. She was certain that Sally and the other girls resented the idea of her leaving. And, if she didn't leave after all, would they still resent her? After all, it was Stacey who was singled out. She was invited to the other team. But then again, neither Sally, Bobbie Rose, nor Pam ever expressed any strong desire to do more than just play the school matches. They never entered the state tournaments or any tournaments for that matter. So maybe I'm imagining too many things? thought Stacey.

A moment later, she picked off a flat serve and returned it deep to Sally's forehand. There was a rapid exchange as both players strained to make the approach shot. Finally, Stacey hit a wild backhand that sailed out of the court by ten feet.

"Just out by inches," shouted Sally, trying to be funny.

But Stacey wasn't listening. For the first time that she could remember, her body was aching severely. There was pain in her neck muscles. There was pain in her lower back. She wanted to walk off the court, jump into the ocean, and float on her back in the salt water.

"Okay, it's five o'clock," Lee Goodman yelled. "Let's call it a day."

"A day," whispered Pam to Stacey as the players walked toward the grim-faced coach.

"We have a tough match on Friday against Gatley," the coach said. "So I've scheduled four hour sessions every day for the rest of the week."

There were groans from Bobbie Rose and Sally. Carrie and Shirl turned around and glanced at Stacey. They smiled shyly, indicating a pleasurable excitement.

Stacey, at fifteen, felt like an old pro when she was around the newcomers. The girls were openly enthusiastic about being on the varsity squad. They looked to Stacey as the leader, the one local player who'd competed in the "biggies down south," in Miami and Fort Lauderdale.

"Edison! Walker! Pay attention," said the coach, and the girls turned away from Stacey and looked dutifully at Lee Goodman. "I haven't made up the assignments for the Gatley match but don't worry about it. You'll probably all get a chance to play."

Stacey walked over to the bench, sat down heavily, and threw a towel around her neck. As she packed her racquets, the significance of Coach Goodman's words was obvious. She had not made the assignments because Stacey was a question mark.

"Going home?" asked Pam.

"Never," Stacey answered, letting the towel fall over her face.

The remark startled Pam. She lifted the front of Stacey's towel, revealing a weary face.

"Just kidding, Hayward. But I think I'll go for a quick dip."

Pam nodded and walked away.

Stacey went into the locker room, threw her sweaty clothes into a laundry bag, and put on a black bathing suit. The place was quiet, as usual. The team preferred, as did Stacey, to take showers in their own homes. Stacey slipped a hooded sweatshirt over her swimsuit, picked up her tennis and laundry bags, and headed for Pelican Beach.

As she walked the two blocks, she kept hearing the encouraging voices of Keith, Pam, Michael, and her father being drowned out by Sally, Wally, and her mother. The words got all jumbled, resulting in one massive headache. Her lower back was hurting again. Her neck was throbbing with pain. Letting out a moan, she ran along the white sand, dropping her two bags midway to the water. Without breaking stride, she dove headfirst into a late-breaking wave.

With her head facedown, she swam directly out, being pushed back by the waves, then plowing ahead for several hundred yards. When she turned over onto her back, the waters were calm. Stacey floated for what seemed to be a long time, letting the late afternoon sun warm her face. The salt water soothed her nerves. Finally she' looked around. There was another person in the water. He was about seventy feet away. Treading water and breathing deeply, she recognized the now-familiar solitary surfer. He was practicing three-hundred-and-sixty-degree turns as he rode a wave toward the shore. Each attempt was followed by a spill, which was followed by determined paddling back out to try again. After three attempts, the surfer finally made his full turn, then rode to shore with his lean arms high over his head in a victory gesture. Instinctively, Stacey began to applaud. As she did, her body momentarily drifted downward. Feeling a little silly, she spat out a mouthful of salty water, then swam hard for shore. A few minutes later, Stacey stumbled to shore. The surfer was still practicing.

"Keep at it," she cried out. "Yeah! Keep at it!"

Stacey knew that the surfer couldn't hear her, but it didn't matter. She felt a kinship with the young man. And she knew that the cry of encouragement was as much for herself as it was for him. She picked up her bags and headed for home.

On Friday, the girls' team and the boys' team had matches against Gatley High. Stacey won her match easily. The pain in her back and neck were gone. But there was a strange tension in the air.

Maybe I'm imagining things, thought Stacey. My teammates are friendly enough. But it's like they're waiting for me to say something. What do they want from me? What do I want from myself?

"I'm going over to watch the guys play," Stacey told Pam, perhaps a bit too casually.

Pam smiled conspiratorially and winked.

"Checking things out, huh?" she whispered. "I'll see you over there later."

It was a warm day. The sun bore down heavily on Stacey's back as she strolled across the field to the school's other tennis courts. She was still wearing her clothes from the match. The only addition was a white towel wrapped around her neck. A sudden breeze kicked up. Stacey reached into her tennis bag and pulled out the blue and orange team jacket.

She sat in the stands and watched the Jones brothers lose their doubles match. Stacey could not concentrate. Her mind was wandering — wondering why the girls never got to play on these asphalt courts in the pretty, compact mini-stadium with its ten rows of gleaming blue seats? Or where Keith Flowers was at this very moment? She got her answer in the next five minutes. The doubles match was concluded. Stan and Chuck walked off the court sheepishly. They both shrugged their shoulders at Coach Albertson, who said a few words to them. Then the coach spotted Stacey and waved. He was accustomed to seeing her at the team matches, but Albertson made it a point not to talk to Stacey. Without being unfriendly, he remained polite and aloof. Any decision would have to come from Stacey without his influence or Lee Goodman's. Keith walked onto the court bouncing lightly on the balls of his feet. He wore a simple all-white outfit.

So he would be my future teammate, Stacey mused, when and if. . . .

She unconsciously tucked her yellow tennis blouse into her blue skirt, then straightened and smoothed her outfit. Keith looked up and smiled. Stacey smiled back, then put the towel over her head. Seventy minutes later, Keith had won his match. His white outfit still looked spotless.

Stacey had watched the entire match, unaware that Van Larsen, Chuck and Stan Jones were sitting behind her. It was only when Pam appeared at the end of the match, suddenly there beside her, that Stacey turned around. Van clapped his hands and was immediately joined by the Jones brothers.

"Good match, kid," yelled Van.

"Me or Keith?" asked Stacey.

Van started to laugh. He leaned back and stretched his legs.

"Not you, dummy. Pam Hayward."

"But I lost my match," said Pam, frowning and shaking her head.

"In that case," said Van, "forget it."

Pam and Stacey sat down and exchanged knowing looks.

"That Larsen is a creep," whispered Pam. "He's always saying and doing dumb things."

"But he *is* a good player," said Stacey.

"So what?" asked Pam. "So who cares? Does that give him the right to be an idiot?"

"No," said Stacey. "I guess you're right. Say — do you remember what I said a long time ago? Like I couldn't imagine doing anything except playing tennis?"

She watched Keith as he huddled with Hank Albertson. Larsen and the Jones brothers now ran down the aisle to the court below.

"So now," said Pam, "you can imagine doing everything except playing tennis? Huh?"

The two friends laughed loudly. Van Larsen scowled at the two girls huddled together in the stands.

"I want to play more than ever," said Stacey, suddenly serious. "In fact, I really

feel secure and confident on the court. It's
. . . just off the court that can be a problem.
Some of these Neptune boys leave something
to be desired."

Stacey was not really saying what was on
her mind. Wally Baxter had called earlier in
the week and asked her out for Saturday
night. Stacey had said yes, but without en-
thusiasm. There was going to be a party at
Dave Kelly's house, so Pam would be there.
Sally and Van were coming. There would be
other couples. Stacey was finally dating. She
was finally in a "social circle." But, somehow,
the dating scene didn't have the excitement
of a big tennis tournament in Fort Lauderdale. Something was missing. Someone was
missing. Not that Wally was such a bad person. He was just self-absorbed. But maybe
I'm too self-absorbed Stacey thought.

"Did you get to see any of this last match?"
she asked Pam. "Keith was really excellent.
He plays such a smart game. He's always in
the right position, always ready. Wow! He
really knows the game."

Pam studied her friend's face.

"Yeah," she said, "and he's cute, too."

Stacey laughed, a little too loudly.

"Am I blushing?" she asked.

"Can't tell," said Pam. "Could be from the
sun. Could be from something else."

Keith was walking up the aisle toward
them. Pam stood up quickly and moved away.

"Got to go," she said. "Dave and I are
studying together."

"Oh yeah sure," said Keith. "Is that what they call it?"

"You're as funny as Van Larsen," said Pam, waving goodbye to Stacey.

There was a strange silence as Stacey tried to focus on her friend as she bounded down the steps, two at a time.

Time for me to leave, thought Stacey. Things to do; things to do. Have to talk to . . . someone.

"You always mumble like that?" asked Keith. "Oh yes, you do. You know that, don't you?"

Stacey grinned and nodded her head vigorously.

"You look like a Moroccan woman," commented Keith, "with that towel over you like that."

"Like what?"

Keith reached forward and fingered the thick white towel.

"Like . . . that," he said.

Stacey wanted to ask him where Debby Klinger was — if she'd be taking pictures with her little camera? Or if he'd be coming to Dave Kelly's party with that sensational dancer, Jackie Girard? But Stacey knew that any remark would be catty, that she really didn't care about Keith Flower's girl friends. She bit her lip.

"I have to tell you something," said Keith, and his warm blue eyes made Stacey wrap the towel even tighter around her neck.

"I saw your match against Lola Anderson

from Gatley. You were sensational. No kidding. You are one heavy hitter. Very tough. Very impressive."

All Stacey could do was nod her head over and over again, like a wind-up doll.

"Thank you," she said, finally. "Thank you very much. Ummm, and I like the way you play. I was just watching . . . your match."

Keith drew back into himself. It was almost as if a curtain had come down between them. Stacey barely understood what was happening.

"See you," said Keith.

He turned and ran lightly down the steps.

"Oh yes," said Stacey, half to herself, "I like the way you play. I was just . . . watching. . . ."

Suddenly her head was very clear. There was no Keith, no Pam, no one except Stacey King sitting alone, looking down onto an empty tennis court. She knew what she had to do. All the conversations, all the worry, all the questioning and self-doubt were swept away. She took off her towel and threw it into her tennis bag. Then she began the long walk back across the field to Hank Albertson's office.

Stacey King had decided. She was ready to join the Neptune High School boys' tennis team!

E^{ight}

It was a time for celebration. Lucinda King spent all day Saturday preparing a shrimp jambalaya, with onions and green peppers. Michael took it upon himself to prepare the roux, a special Cajun hot sauce. It was a mix of flour, oil, and hot spices used for thickening purposes. In the King family, everybody cooked; everybody shared the housework. Stacey was barred from all housework today, in honor of finally joining the boys' team — she was queen for the day.

"I can live with it," said Stacey, going through her wardrobe. "For one glorious day, I'll be a King and a queen," she quipped.

Michael guffawed loudly. Then he walked out of the room, whistling the violin part of a Mozart concerto.

"Hold the noise down," shouted Stacey. "I'm trying to concentrate. Have to look beautiful for my big Saturday night date."

She selected a pink and white dress with a short hemline.

Only question is, pondered Stacey, does it make me look too little-girlish?

She tried it on. With its scooped neck, the dress definitely had possibilities. Stacey added rhinestone earrings, which dangled and sparkled in the late afternoon sunshine streaming through the window. A touch of lipstick, perhaps? A little eyeliner? A dab of — Stacey stood in front of the mirror. She tossed the lipstick in the air, deftly caught it with one hand, then repeated the gesture.

What am I trying to prove? she asked herself. Just because I'm now on the boys' team, do I have to come on strong so everyone knows I'm really and truly a girl? Or maybe I just want to wear makeup?

Finally she applied Magic Crimson to her puckered lips. It tasted good. Stacey stepped back — she looked good. A little weird, seeing herself that way, but it was okay. Next, she tried a bit of blush, smoothing it below her wide cheekbones like she had seen Sally and Bobbie Rose doing so many times.

A pair of high-heeled white sandals stood at attention below her. Stacey slid into them, wobbling just a little as she stepped back to inspect herself. After a lifetime of wearing sneakers, any other kind of shoe was strange, but these seemed particularly awkward.

I think I look pretty all right, Stacey concluded. But the next moment she felt like a little girl masquerading as a grown-up woman.

Two hours later when she made her entrance into the dining room, Bill King gasped, then nodded his head approvingly. Her mother rubbed away a smudge of blush, improving Stacey's appearance. Michael just whistled.

"My kid sister's come of age," he said. "Definitely worthy of big-time tennis."

Stacey was glad that no one made any further mention of the boys' team. She had their support, that was all that mattered. If it had been otherwise, she still would have gone through with her decision. But her family's backing made everything easier. She was ready for the shrimp jambalaya. She was ready for Wally Baxter and the Saturday night party.

First there was a movie, Wally insisted they see an old French film called *Jules and Jim*, about two friends in love with the same woman. Stacey sighed heavily.

"It's all about love and friendship," explained Wally.

"Well," said Stacey, disconsolately, "I'm always willing to learn about love and friendship. And maybe I can improve my French. Mr. Rosenthal says I don't have a feeling for the language."

She sat in the dark theater, like a model in her pretty pink and white dress, rigidly at attention so that the dress wouldn't get any creases. Wally said nothing about her dress, her earrings, or her makeup. For all that it mattered, this big hulk could have gone to the movies alone. Finally, mercifully, it was over.

"Well, how'd you like it?" asked Wally, his chest filled with pride. "I think it's important for two people to share an artistic experience."

"I wouldn't exactly call that an artistic experience," said Stacey. "Frankly, I couldn't see what those two guys saw in her. She wasn't pretty. She just hung around and sulked and pouted. Pretty boring stuff."

They walked side by side to the parking lot. Wally's face was all twisted, which Stacey supposed was an indication of deep thought.

"But they were all close," he insisted. "They communicated with each other, even if it wasn't always through words."

"Well," said Stacey, "I like to communicate through words. It's called talking. Works pretty well in our family."

She just wanted to get to the party. Her shoes felt a little tight but Stacey didn't care. She was ready to rock and roll.

"You know," said Wally, "you hardly ever talk."

Stacey wanted to take off her shoes and hit Wally Baxter over the head. Hardly ever talk!, she silently fumed. This big deal senior does all the talking for both of us. Can't get a word in edgewise.

They continued walking to the car. As Wally opened the passenger door, Stacey spoke up, breaking the tense silence.

"I joined the boys' tennis team."

Wally stood there, the door open, his mouth open, the car keys dangling limply in his hand. Someone called out his name from the small crowd. He did not turn around.

"Big mistake," he said, finally. "And you totally disregarded my advice."

He slammed the door shut. Then he shoved the car keys back into his pocket. Wally stalked off to the little park behind the movie theater. Stacey hobbled after him, vowing never to wear high heels again.

"Come on, Wally, let's go to the party. It'll take your mind off my *shameful* decision."

Stacey's sense of humor was lost on Wally. He walked quickly through the crowds like a downfield runner eluding would-be tacklers. She followed her football star to the duck pond in the middle of the small park.

"Hey, ease up," she shouted. "I can't run after you in high heels."

He turned around at the edge of the water. A duck honked behind him. Stacey wanted to laugh. But she did contain herself, smoothing would-be wrinkles out of her dress. Then she stepped out of her shoes and breathed a sigh of relief as her stockinged feet touched the grass.

"Okay, Wally. Now will you communicate?"

"First of all, let me say that the reason I wanted to come to the duck pond was because it's quiet. I didn't want us to start shouting in a crowd. I know a lot of those people."

His mouth opened wide, but Stacey interrupted. Her neck felt warm, like a midday sun was beating on it. She picked up her shoes and clutched them.

"I wasn't about to start shouting," said Stacey. "Speak for yourself."

Wally stared past her.

"How is it going to look," he said, "for me to be dating a member of the boys' tennis team?"

"That's what you're concerned about? What people are going to think?"

"I've got a reputation," said Wally, "a good reputation."

He took one big step to the edge of the pond. He squatted, staring all the while at a brownish duck. The bird looked suspiciously at Wally, then paddled away.

"And don't tell me that you don't care what people think," argued Wally. "You were plenty concerned. And I'll bet you still are."

"Sure I was concerned," said Stacey. "That's why it took me so long to make up my mind. I had a lot of things to consider."

"So. . . . ?"

"So I considered them," said Stacey, "and

then I made up my own mind. My . . . own . . . mind."

Wally didn't answer and neither of them spoke for a few minutes.

"You know," said Wally, breaking the long silence, "I was thinking of taking you to the Orange Crush next month."

Stacey found herself getting excited, almost in spite of herself. The Orange Crush was *the* social event of the year for Neptune High's athletes. The school arranged to have a section of the beach roped off. There was live music, refreshments, and a big platform for dancing. If there were no jellyfish or sharks, a lot of the kids went swimming. Stacey had never been asked. It was one event where she clearly understood that a date was required.

"It would be pretty ridiculous," continued Wally, resuming his cruising speed, "if I got a reputation for dating a member of the boys' tennis team."

"I'm still a girl."

"You wouldn't catch a boy playing on the girls' team," argued Wally.

Stacey sucked in air, then slowly exhaled. She focused on the smug profile of Wally Baxter.

"Can't think of a reason for a boy to play on the girls' team," said Stacey. "But you know perfectly well why Coach Albertson wants me on the team. And Lee Goodman backs him up."

"I still don't like it," said Wally.

107

"Well then," snapped Stacey, "you can go take a bona fide member of the Girls' team to the Orange Crush. There are two new freshmen. Or maybe I should say — freshwomen? They'd be thrilled to be asked, I'm sure."

"Hey," shouted Wally, "you get on the big deal boys' team and you turn into a wise guy."

Stacey folded her arms and tightened her lips as the car pulled into a small driveway. The ranch-style house was an imitation of southwest Spanish ranch houses. But this place, thought Stacey, looks like a good stiff wind would blow it away. Maybe it'll take Wally Baxter with it.

Stacey was quiet during the two hours she and Wally spent at the party. She did dance with him but there was no joy in her dancing. Pam and Sally were there but no one was in a conversational mood. Everyone was bobbing and boogying and rocking around the pool and on the patio. Just before midnight, Bobbie Rose fell into the pool.

"I don't know where my head was," Bobbie Rose said when she got out. "I was looking up at the stars, I guess."

"Good thing there was water in the pool," said Pam, "or you would have been seeing stars for a long, long time."

The boys were in the kitchen, arguing about the new football and basketball teams. Stacey ran to the bathroom, found a large towel, then ran back out to the shivering Bobbie Rose.

All the girls were laughing now, including Bobbie Rose. Stacey simply shook her head as she vigorously rubbed Bobbie's black hair. The girl reminded her of a wet poodle. Cute, but wet.

"I want to tell you all something," said Stacey.

Sally rushed forward, waving a green terry-cloth bathrobe.

"Wait a sec," she yelled. "I found the perfect outfit for this Olympic swimmer. And you return it, Bobbie. Dave says it's his mother's favorite."

"It's ten sizes too big for me," complained Bobbie Rose.

A groan went up from the three girls.

"But I'll take it," continued Bobbie Rose.

Bobbie was still towelling off as Stacey spoke above the laughter.

"Let me tell you: I decided. I joined the boys' team yesterday. I report for my first practice on Monday afternoon. Well? What do you think?"

For a long moment, the three girls looked at one another. Then Pam hugged Stacey.

"This is your life, Stacey King. It's going to be a great experience. Just don't forget your old friends."

Stacey grimaced as she blushed.

"Come off it," she said. "I'm playing with you tomorrow. And we'll still play doubles in the big tournaments down south."

"But not the school tournaments," said Sally, in an even voice.

Sally managed a smile, as did Bobbie Rose. Stacey sensed an awkwardness and a drawing back on the part of the two girls. Or was that only her imagination? Certainly Pam was pleased; her best friend usually did understand Stacey. But there was nothing she could do about Sally and Bobbie. Stacey wanted them to be happy for her or, at least, to realize the situation.

"You're good now," said Sally. "I still don't see why you want to cause all this trouble just for a little self-improvement. And there will be trouble."

Van Larsen came out at that precise moment, combing his hair.

"What's all this about causing trouble? Who's causing trouble? What kind of trouble? What's. . . . ?"

Sally broke the news, and Van's face opened quickly into an even wider grin than usual.

"Congrats, kid," he said. "Maybe you'll be the new number one on the team!"

His eyes were twinkling. Stacey smiled back.

"Coach Albertson has a ranking system," explained Van. "We compete against each other as well as other teams. So all you have to do is beat me . . . and the Jones boys . . . and you know who."

"Come on, Van, all I'm going to be doing

is trying to upgrade my game. Your number two status is safe and secure."

Keith Flowers walked out to the pool area. He had just arrived at the party. Stacey thought he looked great in his blue and white Hawaiian shirt with large zig-zag patterns. He wore a white jacket over the shirt. Stacey wondered where Debby Klinger was — or Jackie Girard.

"Hey, Keith," shouted Van, "meet our new teammate."

He pointed a thumb at Stacey, as the tall athlete came toward her. Stacey felt like a huge toy doll on display. Both Sally and Bobbie Rose were silently questioning her. Their frowns implied a painful criticism. But Keith's blue eyes were soft and gentle, immediately relaxing her, indicating that everything was all right. He seemed to understand without any need for explanations. In that brief moment, in that one direct look, Stacey saw a sensitive, accepting individual. Unlike Sally and Bobbie Rose, Keith appeared to be unconcerned with making judgments. Yet Stacey felt like explaining. Or maybe it was just that she felt like talking to him? Or simply being with him?

"What's going on?" asked Keith, with a sudden intensity.

"What do you mean?" gasped Stacey, self-consciously.

Keith turned to Bobbie Rose and flashed a sparkling smile, shaking his head sympathetically.

"Bobbie, you'd better get home and dry off," said Keith. "You're going to catch a real bad cold. Go on; get going."

For one fleeting, nightmarish moment, Stacey had felt that she was going to be ridiculed. Now she exhaled a sigh of relief. But why did she care what Keith thought or said? He was nice. He was more than nice. But he was clearly interested in any number of girls, none of whom included Stacey King.

"I'll get going if you take me home," said Bobbie Rose, flirtatiously. "But you have to dump that harem of yours."

Immediately there was raucous laughter around the pool. Even Keith was amused, shaking his head and throwing up his hands in a helpless gesture. All the noise brought Dave Kelly and Wally Baxter out of the kitchen.

"What did we miss?" asked Dave. "Somebody tell a good joke?"

"So what was so funny?" asked Wally, scratching his chest.

Stacey walked along the edge of the pool. She looked at Keith's reflection. He was staring into the still, green water. Then Stacey tossed a penny into the pool, near his feet. The slight rippling effect distorted Keith's face.

"You about ready to go home?" asked Wally.

"Huh? Oh yeah, sure. I'm about ready."

"I guess I didn't spend much time with you," Wally whispered. "I got into a heavy discussion with Dave. Sorry."

Stacey tossed another penny into the pool, watching it sink quickly to the bottom. The faint splash made Keith look up.

"Don't throw your good money away," he cautioned.

"They're only pennies," answered Stacey.

Then she turned and walked away with her big Saturday night date. It was too confusing. She appreciated Wally's apology. But it may have come too late. Or perhaps it didn't matter at all? Perhaps all of this dating business was overrated. The one sure thing that Stacey could count on was that wonderful game called tennis. She was moving up. Boys' team, girls' team — it didn't make any difference to her.

Let them call me a machine, thought Stacey. Tennis maiden, tennis machine, it makes no difference what they say. I've got what I want.

As Wally talked on and on, behind the wheel of his not-quite speeding car, the wind blew her hair, and Stacey couldn't erase the image of Keith Flowers standing alone at the side of the dark, quiet pool.

Nine

Sometime between eleven PM Sunday night and six AM Monday morning, Stacey had a dream. She was standing on a narrow, wooden tennis court that revealed itself (in a fuzzy aquamarine way) to be part of Hermosa Pier. Across the net were Wally, Keith, Van, Sally, and Bobbie Rose. There were also faceless players standing behind them. A ball floated toward Stacey. It was the size of a grapefruit. Stacey tried to run toward it, but her legs refused to move! When she finally reached the large, pinkish sphere, Stacey tried to swing her racquet, but it was too heavy for her to wield. Then she saw that the racquet had no strings. Her brother, her mother, and her father were all silently shouting. Stacey dragged the heavy racquet along the pier, all the time straining to hear what her family was saying, and then they were gone. She turned and moved somehow, toward the net, toward her friends across the court. They were gesturing for her to come over — but the net grew higher and higher. Stacey dropped her racquet and tried to climb over it, but she couldn't get a toe-hold. Then she tried to crawl under the net, but she couldn't lift it. Then she moved toward the sidelines, hoping to get around to the other side. However, the strangely growing net extended on both sides to the very edge of the pier and out over the water!

Stacey woke up crying. For a time, she didn't know if she was still in the dream or awake. She brushed away the tears, not knowing why she had cried. She tried to fall back asleep, then she sighed heavily and got out of bed.

Stacey stepped out into the backyard. Her bare feet touched the manicured lawn wet from the morning dew. A nervous sparrow darted away and landed at the far end of the grassy plot and began pecking for insects.

"I'm hungry," announced Stacey. "Food! I need food."

But she lingered, breathing in the cool, fresh air. The dream receded in her mind as the mindless comfort of routine took over. Stacey prepared a breakfast of fresh grapefruit, bananas, and cereal with milk. By the time she finished washing the dishes, her mother and father were staggering along the hall, half-asleep.

"Kind of early for you," her mother said.

"Yeah," said Stacey. "Big day, I guess."

"Good luck," her mother said, moving past and kissing Stacey on the cheek.

Bill King was totally uncommunicative until he'd showered and had his mug of coffee. He did manage to kiss his daughter as he shuffled into the kitchen.

Now Stacey was anxious to get out. Today was going to be an important day. She had tried not to think about it. Certainly she had not talked any more about it with Pam. There had been such a build-up, so much talk, anxious stares, and unanswered questions that Stacey was tired of the whole business. She just wanted to get on with her life, be a part of the school community. Quickly, carefully, she checked the strings of her racquets, then packed them.

She looked at her watch. It was all of seven o'clock. Her first class, French, would not be starting for another hour.

"*Quel fromage,*" she sighed. "I mean, *quel domage. Bon jour,* Monsieur Rosenthal."

"Hey, kiddo," yelled Michael from outside the door, "you going crazy? Only crazies talk to themselves."

Stacey opened the door.

"Ah, *bon jour, mon frere,*" she sang.

"Hey, today's the big day," said Michael, "good luck. I mean, *bon chance.*"

Stacey threw her tennis bag over her shoulder, then grabbed her school books.

"*Merci beaucoup,*" she said. "Thank you. I'll try to live up to the great name of King."

"Just keep your eye on the ball," said Michael.

"Okay, coach," Stacey said, tapping him on the shoulder and skipping out the door.

Stacey did not take the bike. Instead, she walked the quarter mile to Neptune High. It was a good time to be up, Stacey decided. At that early hour, there were no reminders of winning or losing matches, dating or not dating boys. There was just a salty breeze off the ocean and a hazy sun beginning to climb in the pale blue sky.

By the time Stacey arrived at the old concrete structure that was Neptune High, it was seven thirty. She looked up at the building and shook her head critically. What a dump, she thought. Not the most inspiring place in the world. Looks more like a prison. A familiar voice turned her around.

"Hey, Stacey King, what brings you here at this early hour?"

It was Keith Flowers. He was running in place and perspiring heavily.

"I didn't know you ran," she said. "No wonder you're in such good shape."

"We'll have to go running some time," he said, gasping for breath.

"Sure," said Stacey, surprised and excited at the same time. "Now that we're teammates. . . ."

"See you later," said Keith, running away toward the track field.

Before she could collect her thoughts, Wally Baxter was jogging toward her.

"Sure is a busy place," said Stacey, grinning broadly.

"You and Keith always meet here?" asked Wally.

He stopped directly in front of Stacey, looking like a highway patrolman about to give a ticket for speeding.

"Oh, come on, Wally, it's too early in the morning for this kind of a scene."

"Well, I want to know if we're going to the Orange Crush."

Stacey had been hearing about this big social event for weeks. As far as she was concerned, it was just another party. She couldn't understand the fuss over dancing on the beach.

"Do we have to discuss this right now?" asked Stacey, wearily. "I've got a lot to do. And I want to relax. I want to enjoy my classes."

"I know it's your big day," said Wally, backing down. "I mean, it's not every day that a girl gets to play with the boys."

Stacey walked over to the front steps of the main building and sat down. Wally, in his running shorts, jogged after her.

"I didn't mean anything by it," he explained. "I just think you're making a big mistake."

"Thanks for your encouraging words," said Stacey.

"I'm trying to be honest," said Wally. "You ought to hear some of your ex-teammates on the subject. Sally and Bobbie Rose think

118

you're going to ruin the whole school system."

"Oh yeah? Well, I don't care what anybody thinks."

Wally shrugged his massive shoulders, then waved sheepishly and ran off toward the gymnasium. Stacey hunched forward, slapping her hands nervously. Who else is going to run by? she wondered. Who else is going to make my day?

Familiar faces began to appear, riding by on bikes, walking past. There was Julia De Diego, sparkling as if she'd just stepped out of a shower.

"Hey, Julia, *como estás*?"

"Speak English, gringo," Julia shouted with a grin. "How was your weekend?"

"Oh," said Stacey, affecting a bored attitude, "nothing but parties, parties, and more parties."

"Yeah, I know what you mean," said Julia. "My weekend was pretty boring, too. See you later."

A thought crept into Stacey's head. How will Julia feel when she finds out Stacey King is playing on the boys' team? Why should it matter?

She stood up and stretched her arms to the puffy clouds overhead. It was time for French, for computer math, for American history, for English literature. It was time for the reality of school.

Neptune High School was neatly laid out.

Strolling from left to right, a visitor could walk past the parking lot to the main school building to the main gymnasium building (which contained locker rooms for all the athletes) to the track field. At the end of the line, past the cinder track oval, was the boys' tennis courts with their small, sturdy grandstand. The girls' tennis courts, with their rickety old grandstand were like an afterthought. They broke the neat architectural line. These courts were situated northwest of the track field, diagonally across from the main gym. Getting there was a trek.

At two o'clock, Stacey was in the locker room, changing into white tennis shorts and a pale blue shirt. She had a certain ritual, deciding which of several wrist bands to wear. Finally, she selected a bright red one.

All the girls from the team were changing into their tennis clothes at that moment. Sally and Bobbie Rose both sneaked looks at Stacey. They tried to affect an indifference to her. The younger players, Shirl Walker and Carrie Edison, were openly staring at Stacey with expressions of ingenuous admiration on their faces.

"So how do you feel?" asked Pam. "Big workout today!"

"I guess I'm excited," said Stacey.

"Well, good luck," said her friend. "Play well."

"Thanks."

Stacey laced her sneakers, picked up her tennis racquets, and walked past Sally and

Bobbie Rose. The girls nodded and flashed quick smiles.

"You're the talk of the school," muttered Sally. "Everybody in the cafeteria wanted to know when you're playing your first match."

Stacey shrugged her shoulders.

"That's up to Coach Albertson," she said. "I have to earn the right to play."

"Oh, I'm sure you will," broke in Carrie Edison. "I think you can beat Keith Flowers right now."

Sally's mouth fell open in disbelief. Stacey and Pam broke out laughing.

"Oh, I'm sure I can't beat Keith," said Stacey.

Sally put on a headband and headed for the exit door. She turned around at the last second and said, "Oh, I'm sure you don't want to beat Keith Flowers. It would end a beautiful relationship before it began."

Then she was gone, followed quickly by Bobbie Rose. There was an uncomfortable silence in the locker room.

"Well," said Pam, "I guess it's nice to know you're the subject of so much gossip."

"Not much I can do about that," muttered Stacey.

"And you and Keith are linked romantically," Pam laughed. "Wonderful. We can all read about you in *People* magazine."

"Oh yeah?" gasped Shirl Walker. "That's neat!"

"That's only a joke, dummy," Carrie Edison said. "Don't take everything so seriously."

Stacey and Pam looked at each other as if to say, "Kids, what can you do!" Then they exchanged parting smiles as Stacey headed out the door.

Didn't know tennis was such a popular sport, Stacey thought. But it still hasn't got gossiping beat as the number one sport.

When Stacey stepped onto the tennis court, Hank Albertson greeted her with a wave of his cap.

"Welcome to the squad," he said. "Glad to have you aboard."

Wow! thought Stacey. Sounds like a ship's captain greeting a sailor.

She took a deep breath, then nodded quickly to her new teammates sitting in a row on a long bench. Stacey was not the only new player. There was a frail, smallish boy who couldn't have been more than five feet seven. His name was Marcel Philippe and he was from Haiti. His power was deceptive. Hank Albertson had spotted him playing with his father at Neptune's public court. The boy's strength was in his timing, in a whiplike action that utilized all of his thin frame.

"Okay, fellows," announced Albertson. "Er, I mean fellows and girl."

Everyone chuckled, including Stacey.

"For the benefit of our newcomers," continued Albertson, "I want to say a few words about our ranking system. In the interest of

122

fairness, we'll have intersquad contests. Along with the outside matches, the seven schools we have yet to play, the combination of wins and losses will determine the number one player. In the event of a tie, I'll make the final selection. This is all to let you know that I won't be playing favorites. You'll all be judged strictly on your merit."

"Well, I guess that leaves me out," Van Larsen joked.

Only the Jones brothers laughed. The coach fixed his number two player with a stare that wiped the smirk off his face.

"And I don't want you playboys making any social dates for the weekend of the fifteenth," lectured the coach. "That's the big tournament in Fort Lauderdale. For the benefit of our newcomers . . . " He paused and smiled down at Stacey and the wide-eyed Marcel Philippe.

". . . that's the Sunshine Bowl — where the top schools from each district compete in a statewide contest. Neptune seems to be doing well, so far, in our district."

Stacey noted that the coach grimaced when he said, "so far." She knew about the Sunshine Bowl, of course. Her heart beat just a little bit faster as she pictured herself in the middle of all that tennis talent. Even if she didn't compete, it would be a thrill to see those athletes in action. And if, by chance. . . .

Stacey did not like to dwell on possibilities. She would take each game, each set, each match — moment by moment by moment.

"So I want all you playboys to maintain our good record," barked Albertson.

"What about play*girls*?" asked Van Larsen.

Everyone laughed now, including Stacey.

"Larsen," said the coach, "for a change, you're right. Hey, Stacey, welcome to the team."

She was glowing. Immediately Stacey turned to the blushing Marcel and introduced herself. He mumbled a hello with the trace of a French accent.

"My name is Stacey King."

"I am Marcel Philippe."

"You speak French?" asked Stacey.

The boy nodded.

"*Je suis enchante de faire votre connaisance,*" she said, proudly.

"I was born in Miami," he whispered. "I prefer to speak English."

Stacey grinned, then shrugged her shoulders. Okay for you, she thought, I guess that put me in my place.

The workout went well for Stacey. Albertson matched her against all of the players, for twenty-minute periods. She instantly enjoyed the challenge of hitting against the other boys. The frail Marcel amazed her. Although he lacked steadiness, the boy hit with a looping topspin that kept Stacey planted back at the baseline. But she derived her greatest satisfaction from hitting with

124

Keith. Stacey could really appreciate the young man's skills and intelligence. Of course there was a degree of tension. She knew she was being judged by the players and by the coach. But she was aware of her abilities. On the court, there was none of the shyness and reserve that characterized so much of her dating behavior. There was no Wally Baxter to deal with. Chuck Jones behaved in such an amiable manner, shouting words of encouragement across the net, that Stacey did not think about their awkward evening together. Coach Albertson was proving himself right. When she practiced with Van and Keith, these two excellent players brought out the best in her game. The better each of them played, the more Stacey hit with power and control. She knew instantly that she would only do better with each fresh challenge.

After the workout, Van Larsen casually invited Stacey to a country music concert on Friday night.

"It's going to be great," said Van. "You know who's playing? Wendell Vose and his Good Ol' Boys. Vose used to be a stock car racer. The man's crazy. But good."

"I have one of his tapes," said Stacey. "I'm always playing it at Runaway Beach. It puts me in a real relaxed frame of mind."

"Excellent," said Van. "I like my dates in a real relaxed frame of mind."

The players were all headed for the locker

room. Van turned and began walking away.

"Uh, Van, what about Sally?" Stacey said. "I thought you two. . . . ?"

"Hey, it's not like we're going steady or anything. Besides, this is just a friendly date. Unless you think Wally Baxter would blow a fuse?"

Stacey removed her wristband and put it in her pocket. Then she winked at Van.

"Hey," she said, mimicking him, "it's not like we're going steady. Or anything."

"All right," he said, "I'll pick you up at seven." Then, with a grin, he added, "And wear something . . . country. Gets you in the proper spirit of the evening."

"Okay. Thanks for telling me," said Stacey. "Anyway, I'll see you tomorrow at practice."

"Oh yeah, sure," said Van. "Almost forgot."

"And wear something . . . tennisy," she said with a smile. "Gets you in the proper spirit of the workout."

Van laughed, pointed a finger at Stacey, and walked away. For a full minute, Stacey stood on the sidelines, holding her tennis bag. Then she began walking the long walk to the main gymnasium, to the locker room. Keith was far ahead. He appeared to be giving a tennis lesson to Marcel Philippe, waving his racquet, and gesturing widely. Van was running quickly to catch up with Coach Albertson. Stacey felt a sense of isolation. She hurried to catch up with the Jones brothers.

"You played real well," said Chuck.

"Yeah, you played real well," said Stan.

"Thank you."

The brothers immediately turned red-faced and hurried along the grass. Stacey suppressed a giggle. The Jones boys seemed to do everything exactly alike. They even walked the same way.

Stacey decided to take a shower before going home. The locker room was deserted. But, when she had finished showering and stepped out with a big towel around her, Bobbie Rose was there.

"How did it go today?" she asked.

"Good," said Stacey.

Bobbie nodded uncertainly and left. Stacey did not know what to make of her odd behavior. She figured that it would just take some time before the reality of a girl on the boys' team sunk in. This was going to be the awkward period for a lot of people.

Stacey dressed, packed her tennis gear, and collected her school books. As she was leaving the building, she ran into Keith. He had been silent during the practice session but had watched her intently. She was curious about him. He mostly kept his thoughts and his feelings to himself and yet, when he spoke, there seemed to be genuine concern.

"Big day for you," he said.

"Oh yes. Sure."

"I think you can go all the way in tennis," said Keith. "Make it to the top. No reason why you can't get a national ranking . . . if that's what you want."

They were walking toward the parking lot. She noticed that Debby Klinger was sitting in Keith's white Chevy.

"There are other things in life besides tennis," said Stacey.

"Like what?"

His eyes were totally focused on her. Stacey felt that he was prepared to wait forever for an answer. Now she felt awkward and uncomfortable.

"Oh, there's . . . computers," she began, breaking into a smile. "Truthfully, I'd like to know I could do something besides whack a tennis ball. I'd like to think I had other skills besides good eye-hand coordination."

"What about guys?" asked Keith, blurting out the question before she realized what he was asking. "Or is Wally Baxter the number one guy in your life?"

Stacey could barely breathe. She thought she was back in her dream, unable to move, unable to hear or speak. Her tennis bag felt like it weighed a ton.

"So Wally is number one," Keith said.

Stacey blurted out her reply.

"There is no number one!"

Ten

On Tuesday, Stacey played Chuck Jones in her first intersquad match. She tried to tell herself that there was nothing to worry about, it was only another match. But she was aware of a stiffness in her shoulders and her legs. It was a bright, sunny day so she put sun block on her face and arms. Her hands trembled slightly. She slid a purple wristband onto her right wrist. She retied the laces of her sneakers. Then she strummed the strings of her racquet as if it was a guitar, listening for the ping that indicated the proper stringing, neither too loose nor too tight.

"Ready or not, here I go," she murmured.

Chuck was stretching his legs on the other side of the net, impatient to start playing. He bounced an orange ball with his racquet as Stacey walked uncertainly onto the court.

"Whenever you're ready," he shouted, with a half-smile on his face.

"Okay if we have a little warm-up?" Stacey shouted back.

So they went through the ritual of hitting the ball back and forth from the baseline. Stacey went up to the net to practice her volleys and her overhead. They exchanged practice serves.

"Okay," said Stacey, breathing heavily, "I'm ready if you are."

Chuck spun his racquet on the ground to see who would serve first.

"Up," cried Stacey.

Chuck examined the racquet, then indicated that Stacey's call had been correct. She would serve first.

They both played sloppily during that first game, but Chuck made fewer errors and broke Stacey's serve. During the one-minute rest period, Stacey admonished herself.

"Why am I so uptight?" she asked herself. "I've got nothing to lose. I'm on the team. Nobody expects me to win. So I may as well just play my game.

She immediately relaxed. Stacey took the next six games and won the first set, 6-1. Now the usually mild-mannered Chuck Jones began talking to himself. Coach Albertson watched impassively from the sidelines. The rest of the team drifted over to the benches and sat down. Once again, Stacey felt her back muscles starting to tighten. Nevertheless, she took the second set, 6-4. Chuck Jones barely acknowledged her presence as he walked off the court. Practice was officially over for the day. The players walked off toward the locker room. Only Keith remained behind.

"You played well," he said, "but there was too much tension around your shoulders. Lighten up."

He smiled his gentle smile as he ambled away. Stacey was aware of a sinking sensation in her stomach. Something seemed out of kilter. But what had she expected? Applause? Instant elevation to the number one ranking?

"Am I playing for Keith Flowers or am I playing for myself?" she wondered.

She had applied too much sun block to her forehead. Now it was running over her eyelids. With her wristband, she wiped away the cream, then she adjusted the yellow string around her ponytail.

"Hey kiddo, don't you know it's lonely at the top?"

Stacey shaded her eyes with her left hand as she looked toward the grandstand. She squinted, then picked out a tall, dark figure coming toward her. It was Pam.

"Very impressive victory," she said with a smile. "Get that sour look off your face."

"You're right, you're right," said Stacey. "I guess I'm being too hard on myself. What is it with me? I never used to feel this way."

"I don't know," said Pam, as the two friends strolled easily to their bicycles. "But, if the fun's gone out of the game, it's time to throw away your wristbands."

"What about you?" asked Stacey. "How do you feel these days about playing?"

They pulled their bikes out of the rack but made no effort to ride away. The tennis bag felt heavy on Stacey's shoulders.

"I'm in a different league," said Pam. "I'm not looking to compete in the Sunshine Bowl. I'm not good enough to compete in that kind of league. Sometimes I think I'd like to, but Dave would get upset. Isn't that ridiculous?"

"It sure is," snapped Stacey. "If he can be a big basketball star, why isn't there room for a tennis star? I mean, shouldn't he be proud of you? Shouldn't he encourage you?"

Pam jumped on her bike. For a fleeting second, there were worry lines across her forehead. Then she relaxed and flashed a smile.

"I'm Dave's number one girl friend. That's fine enough with me."

"Well," said Stacey, "I don't think that would be fine enough for me."

That was the end of that conversation. The two friends rode their bikes along the concrete path, lost in their own thoughts.

"See you tomorrow," Pam called, making a sharp turn to the left, and she was gone. Stacey sighed deeply. She knew that she had a lot to learn about boys and about relationships. But in her heart of hearts, she knew that Pam was wrong. There had to be another way. Certainly, Michael and Roberta did not compete with one another. Her brother never spoke of being threatened by his girl friend's musical accomplishments. Were tennis players different? Stacey pointed her bike toward home. There were a lot of questions running around in her head. But there were no answers; not yet.

On Wednesday, Stacey warmed up with Marcel Philippe. He was clearly nervous, which had the effect of relaxing Stacey. Her body moved easily around the court. There were no back pains or leg pains. At one point, Marcel hit three looping shots far beyond the baseline. Stacey motioned for him to come up to the net.

"Marcel," she said in a warm voice, "we're not playing a match. We're just warming up. Take it easy."

"I'm nervous," he said bluntly.

"You don't have to be," said Stacey. "You're on the team. You have nothing to prove."

He shuffled his feet.

"I guess I want to play as well as you," Marcel confessed.

"And I want to play as well as Keith Flowers," said Stacey. "Actually I want to play better than Keith. So where does it end? We can't be instant stars. Just play each moment, each point. Okay?"

"I'll try," he said.

Ten minutes later, they completed their workout. Stacey knew that everything she had said to Marcel applied to herself. There was a normal excitement at the prospect of winning these intersquad matches, but relaxation and concentration were the keys to playing well. She would either win or lose to a superior player. There was no magic formula. Stacey now realized this with a certainty that strengthened her.

She beat Stan Jones, 7-5, 6-3.

Afterwards, Coach Albertson took her aside and casually said he was considering playing Stacey in Neptune's match against Valdosta on Thursday.

"How do you feel about that?" he asked.

Stacey felt like flinging her towel up to the skies. She began skipping toward her bicycle.

"I'm ready, coach," she cried. "No problem."

Albertson winked, then turned to Keith, who was standing nearby.

"Keith here thinks you're the best player on the team," said the silver-haired man.

"I wish he'd tell me that," Stacey blurted out.

There was a mild breeze as the players made their way to the locker room. Stacey dumped her books into the wire basket of her bike, then pushed the bike along the grass as she accompanied Stan and Chuck toward the gray building in the distance. The Jones brothers, affable as they seemed to be at first, now shuffled uncertainly in her presence. They were still pleasant enough, but it was as if they had not been programmed to deal with the reality of a girl on the boys' team, especially a girl who could beat them.

She noticed that Van Larsen, his hands thrust deeply into his team jacket, was walking alone. Stacey hopped on her bike and pedalled toward him. Van appeared to be a bit standoffish.

"Maybe I should be worried about my number two ranking?" he said. "You might be a threat to my reputation." He laughed darkly.

"All I want to know is, are we still on for Friday night?" asked Stacey.

She was surprised at her own bluntness. But why beat around the bush, she figured. Stacey would have asked the same question to Pam or Sally or her brother Michael.

"So what's happening?" she persisted.

"All depends," said Van.

"On what?"

"On how we do against Valdosta on Thursday," he said. "If you play too good, it's too bad. I don't date girls who play better than me."

Stacey had to assume that Van had a good sense of humor.

Suddenly all the energy drained out of her. Stacey got off the bike and sat down on the grass. The warm sun and the faint breeze felt good on her face. Playing well was always satisfying. And winning was the reward. Of course she could play well and lose, but winning was better. Yeah, thought Stacey, it's nice to justify Coach Albertson's faith in me.

Stacey got up slowly and brushed shreds of grass off her white shorts. She rode her bike through the parking lot. Keith Flowers was there in a brightly-colored Hawaiian shirt, lugging his tennis bag toward the white Chevy. Jackie Girard was behind the wheel, loudly honking the horn.

"Let's go, Keith," she cried. "I'm hungry."

"Think beautiful thoughts," he shouted back.

"I can't eat beautiful thoughts," whined Jackie.

Stacey wondered what a guy like Keith was doing with a girl like Jackie. Did he just like to surround himself with beautiful women? Or was there less to Keith Flowers than met the eye?

Keith looked around and saw Stacey. He motioned for her to come over even as Jackie was playing on the car horn, staccato-fashion.

"Jackie, I hear you," said Keith. "Please. I'm talking to a teammate."

"Yeah sure, I'll bet," said Jackie.

He ignored her, then turned his full attention to Stacey.

"You played real well today," he said. "You were definitely 'in the zone!' "

"What's that?" she asked.

"Well, when a tennis player is really hitting in a relaxed way, in a groove, everything falls into place without working at it. So you were in the zone."

The insistent honking of the horn was far away now. There was only the presence of Keith enveloping her. Stacey took a deep breath.

"I think you're always in the zone," she exhaled.

Keith looked past her. His eyes had a misty, faraway look as if he had secret thoughts. Those eyes mystified and intrigued Stacey. She wanted to tell Keith to "lighten up." Instead, she clutched the handlebars of her bike as Keith got into his car. Jackie slid away from him as the white convertible coughed and sputtered, then started. Stacey watched him drive away.

"I wonder if Jackie Girard is in the zone?" she said aloud.

On Thursday, Coach Albertson told Stacey she'd be playing the number four player for Valdosta.

"Great," Stacey said. "I'll be ready."

The brief conversation took place just before nine o'clock as Stacey was about to enter her computer class. For the next four hours, she could barely concentrate on her classes. She flew from room to room. In the cafeteria, Stacey told Pam the exciting news.

"I don't care if Lee Goodman yells at you," said Stacey. "I want you to be there. Wow! What wristband should I wear?"

The two friends giggled, then went their

separate ways. Pam shouted "good luck" as Stacey rushed out the door.

All seven players on the Valdosta team stared blatantly at the entrance of Stacey King onto the number one court. Stacey thought they looked kind of silly, like bowling pins waiting to be knocked over. As one scrawny young man started to leave for the number three court, she could hear him mutter, "Who's the guy with the long hair and the yellow ribbon?" Keith also heard the remark. He was suddenly alongside the Valdosta player, strongly suggesting that the rival player apologize immediately.

"Hey sure," said the grinning athlete, "I was only kidding."

Stacey and Marcel Philippe went to a side court and began warming up. Marcel was in a more relaxed mood on this warm afternoon. He hit with crispness and power. Stacey was amazed at the boy's timing and body rotation, which enabled him to produce such strong shots. It was a good reminder for her to stay calm and just play the game by the book.

Hitting with Marcel was the perfect warm-up for Stacey. She would not try to do anything differently today. A backhand was a backhand; a forehand was a forehand — no matter who was hitting the ball from across the net.

Stacey approached Coach Albertson for his last-minute instructions. She tugged at her skirt, which was now sticking to her perspiring body. She noticed that some of the Valdosta players continued to glance sideways at her.

"You're playing a kid named Billy Freeman," said the coach. "He's got a big serve and nothing else. Crack his serve and he turns to jelly. Okay? Okay!"

Stacy nodded, then slid a maroon band onto her wrist. She retied her yellow ribbon. At that moment, she turned slowly around and looked toward the grandstand. Lee Goodman and the entire girls' team were there. Stacey's former coach and mentor took off her baseball cap and waved it over her head. That had always been Lee Goodman's special "take it easy and win" sign. Stacey waved back. Pam made the thumbs-up sign.

"Okay, Stacey," yelled Albertson. "Get out there. And play a good game, kid."

Stacey was still looking toward the grandstand. Sally and Bobbie Rose were sitting there, stony-faced. An angry feeling rose inside her, but then she saw Michael and their mother smiling at her from the first row. Mrs. King was beaming, but Stacey was not fooled. She knew how nervous her mother was, just before a big match.

So who says this match is big? she asked herself.

"Let's go, Stacey," said Coach Albertson.

Stacey did not play well. She did not break Billy Freeman's serve. She was definitely not "in the zone." Her concentration was not on the ball, not on the game. Rather, stray thoughts kept creeping into her head. What do those Valdosta players think of me? Am I really good enough? What does Keith think of me? Is Sally getting a kick out of this, with that "I told you so" expression? Am I being a disappointment to my mom? To Coach Goodman? How can I justify Coach Albertson's faith in me? Question after question kept popping up. They were meaningless questions, silly questions. And the more she worried about what people thought of her, the worse she played.

Afterwards, her teammates were very supportive. Van said that they were still on for Friday night and that he'd only been kidding before. The Jones brothers were their old, amiable selves. Only Keith remained silent and aloof, looking as downcast as Stacey felt.

That night Stacey went for a long walk along Pelican Beach. At eight o'clock, she wandered over to Hermosa Pier and treated herself to a strawberry yogurt cone. She switched on her cassette player as she walked to the end of the pier. Stacey was about to attach the earplugs of the cassette, to shut out everything except her music, when she felt a tap on her shoulder.

"Looking for Keith Flowers?"

The voice belonged to Sally Llewellyn.

"I'm not looking for anybody," answered Stacey.

"Well, it's common knowledge," said Sally,

"that you're running after him. Debby Klinger and Jackie Girard call him 'Mister Aloof.' They say you're always looking to be with him, that you follow him out to the parking lot. You sure he's not around?"

"The only man I'm here with is my Walkman," said Stacey, putting on her earphones and turning up the volume.

"Well," shouted Sally above the music, "I don't have the opportunity to hang out with the boys. Like *some* people I know!"

"Be my guest," said Stacey. "The more the merrier."

"Provided I'm good enough. Right?"

"Yes, Sally. Provided you're good enough."

Stacey turned her back on Sally. She was more concerned with figuring out the mistakes from her Valdosta match than getting involved with this ridiculous conversation. Stacey slurped on her yogurt cone and left the pier.

On Friday night, Stacey had a perfectly good time with Van Larsen at the country music concert. Wally Baxter was there with a cute blonde who was all over him. That did not prevent Wally from fixing Stacey with a hurt, pained expression.

"Hiya, Wally," shouted Stacey. "Having a good time?"

"Not bad," he shouted back.

Everybody's ridiculous, thought Stacey. If I play tennis, Sally Llewellyn gets uptight. If I go out with a teammate, Wally Baxter gets uptight.

"Hey Van," Stacey said, "I think the number one sport in Neptune is jumping to conclusions."

"Huh?"

"Forget it," said Stacey, turning her full attention to Wendell Vose and his Good Ol' Boys.

It was only when he was driving her home that Van broke the news: Sally Llewellyn had gotten a friend to introduce a "Gender Cross-Over" resolution in the Student Council.

"What's that supposed to mean?" asked Stacey.

"As far as I know," answered Van, "it means that the Student Council would condemn Coach Albertson for having a girl on the team. The Council would recommend that, for the good of school morale, she be removed."

"She being me?" asked Stacey.

"She being you."

Eleven

Stacey was in the kitchen, trying desperately to concentrate on the preparation of a fruit salad. For a full thirty seconds, she held a tiny knife in her hand, staring at a large Golden Delicious apple.

Michael watched her and shook his head sympathetically. He had just finished baking a sourdough bread. While the bread was cooling on a wooden platter, he wiped his forehead.

"Come on, Stace, snap out of it. You look like a statue."

"Oh yes," she replied. "All I need is a little bird on top of my head and you can put me in the park."

She began cutting the apple into little pieces.

"But I think maybe I'm already in the park," she continued. "So many people stare at me now. The last thing in the world that I wanted to be was a public figure."

"Well, I wouldn't exactly call you a public figure," said Michael. "You're not a household word."

He knew what she meant. His sister was the talk of Neptune High School, and not only Neptune. Visiting school teams couldn't wait to see "the girl" in action. Stacey responded angrily to this public notoriety, playing with an intensity that amazed and frightened Coach Albertson and her teammates. Young ladies were not supposed to play with the ferocious aggressiveness that Stacey displayed. She had a booming serve. She rushed the net. She put away overheads and volleys for winners. And she was winning her matches!

Stacey doubled her practice sessions and exercise time, doing more road work, more calisthenics. She had drills and workouts with both Jones brothers on the other side of the net — at the same time.

Van Larsen joked to Keith Flowers that Stacey's "sparring partner," Marcel Philippe, was "losing weight."

"The kid is so obliging," said Van. "He got into the habit of saying yes whenever Stacey wanted him to practice with her. Now he's always got a worried look on his face. I think he may switch to soccer."

Keith was not amused. Daily, he would take Stacey aside and caution her to "lighten up."

"You don't have to prove anything," he said. "And just because some people used to call you a tennis machine. . . . "

Stacey fixed him with a wary look.

". . . doesn't mean you are. Come on, Stacey, it's only a game. It's supposed to be fun."

They were munching on sandwiches in a far corner of the school cafeteria. Stacey stirred her iced tea with a straw, round and round and round.

"The guys from Valdosta don't stare at you," said Stacey.

"I'm not as pretty as you are," said Keith.

The whispered compliment went over Stacey's head. She took a big bite of her egg-salad sandwich, munching it over and over again.

"And the Student Council isn't debating whether or not you should be on the team," said Stacey.

Keith slurped his iced tea, then stood up and grabbed his books and his tennis bag. He had an exasperated expression on his face.

"Traditionally," he began, "boys have always played on boys' teams; girls have always played on girls' teams. You represent a break with tradition. You know that! And you should know that people get nervous with any kind of change."

He stalked off while Stacey chewed on a crust of bread. She knew he was right, and she appreciated his remarks and his genuine concern.

Bridget Salmon and Julia De Diego approached her table. Bridget smiled quickly and kept on walking. Julia immediately sat down.

"Good luck with the Student Council," she said. "I think it's ridiculous that they're even talking about this gender business. Who cares?"

Stacey shrugged her shoulders. She thought of Keith's words as Julia talked on about their computer class. When the first Hispanic families came to Neptune some years ago from Central America, there was a lot of whispering and bad words. But it wasn't long before they were accepted into the community. There was still some pressure — but the situation was certainly calmer now. Julia was just another Neptune teenager. Stacey reminded herself that it was not always so. She would have to put up with a similar kind of pressure.

All week long, there were rumors about the debate in the Student Council. In the hallways, the cafeteria, and in the classrooms, Stacey tried not to mind the questioning stares and the hostile eyes. At the same time she discovered there was a whole body of students who supported her. One day, just before practice, Dave Kelly came over and put his long arm over Stacey's shoulder.

"I've got a buddy on the Council," he said, "and he thinks the whole thing is ridiculous."

"How about you?" asked Stacey.

"As far as I'm concerned," said Dave,

"you can play on the boys' basketball team . . . if you're good enough."

Wally Baxter was polite. He still talked enthusiastically about foreign movies, about football scholarships, and about his athletic skills. He also indicated that the Orange Crush was coming up soon and it would be "a great night." But Wally said nothing about the Gender Cross-Over resolution being debated nor did he ask how Stacey felt. Stacey did not raise the subject.

Late on a Wednesday evening, Stacey and her brother huddled in their backyard, feet dangling over the wall of the canal. A full moon illuminated the still waters. They had been talking about Wally and dating, and boys in general. Stacey picked up a small, flat rock and threw it sideways into the water, watching it skip along the surface.

"Hey, I got four hops out of that rock," said Stacey. "Think you can beat that record?"

"No."

Stacey threw a few more pebbles into the water, watching them skip, counting aloud.

"Well," she said, "I can't say that life is boring. I'm the talk of the school. My name is being thrown around in the Council. I'm going out with Wally from time to time and getting an education in foreign movies. And . . . I've done a little socializing with some of the tennis team."

She felt like adding . . . "except with the

one person I'm really interested in."

"I guess maybe I'd better not fix you up with any more of my friends," said Michael, with a sheepish smile. "Huh?"

"Is that a reference to your buddy, Wally Baxter?" asked Stacey.

Michael slowly nodded.

"Boys don't see boys the way girls see boys," commented Stacey. "You see Wally as a sensitive, caring person. I see him as . . . well, he can be an interesting date but he's so self-involved. It's weird. Wally's different with you than he is with me."

Michael burst out laughing.

"I should hope so," he said.

Stacey was not amused. "Very funny, Mikey, very funny."

"I'm sorry, sis."

His voice had a new tone of respect.

"I think," he continued, "you've grown up a lot in these last couple of months. You're learning about boys and about relationships. I'm impressed."

Stacey eyed him quizzically.

"You don't look impressed, she noted. "In fact, you look downright distracted. Where are you? What's going on?"

Michael laughed nervously. He opened his mouth several times but no words emerged.

The appearance of easy humor and relaxation was conspicuously missing from his face.

"I talk a good game," he said, finally. "I talk about dating like I know what I'm talking about. But I don't know anything. I think maybe I'm like the Wally that you see— self-involved, insensitive. . . ."

His voice trailed off into the evening. He moved away from his sister, raising his shoulders as if to ward off any revealing stares or perceptions from Stacey.

"Michael, what happened?"

"Roberta is mad at me," he said, in a tight voice. "She says I'm never there for her, that I'm losing her, that I'm really dating my violin first and that she's a distant second. I think maybe she's right. I think I better call her right now!"

Michael strode quickly into the house. Stacey looked up to the stars and wondered if she was just like her brother, if she was going steady with her tennis racquet. Maybe this was how Keith and the others saw her, as Miss Tennis Machine.

For a long time, she stood riveted to that one spot, looking up to the stars, shivering in the night, questioning everything about her young life.

On Friday night, Michael was giving a violin concert at the school. The entire King famliy arrived at the auditorium forty minutes early.

"Save me a seat," said Stacey. "I'm just going outside to get some fresh air."

"What's wrong with the air in here?" asked her father.

"Not fresh enough," answered Stacey. "See you in a few minutes."

Stacey stepped outside into the cool evening air. A small crowd had gathered in front of the main building. She tried not to pay attention to the sidelong glances and the whispering students.

"Stacey? Hey, Stacey!"

Stacey turned and was happy to see Roberta Bell's smiling face.

"Big night for your boyfriend," said Stacey. "Everything okay?"

"Oh yes. He's kind of nervous about the Sibelius piece. But, then again, Michael is always uptight before a concert. So I just let him go ahead and worry. I know he'll be fine. And everything's okay."

Roberta seemed to have more to say. Her green eyes kept darting back and forth from Stacey to the crowd. She bit her lower lip.

"So what happening?" asked Stacey, finally. "Something on your mind?"

"I just found out the results of that Gender Cross-Over resolution," said Roberta. "A friend of mine is on the Student Council."

There was a momentary pause. They turned from each other and watched the crowd shuffling into the gray building.

"Good news?" asked Stacey. "Bad news? What? What?"

"Well, it was decided that the issue was not within Council jurisdiction. The vote was split."

"So what does that mean?" asked Stacey.

Her stomach was churning, and she was aware of a slight throbbing sensation in her forehead.

"It means," said Roberta, "that it's a dead issue. From your point of view, you can consider the vote to be a victory. Nobody's going to throw you off the team."

Roberta could still not look Stacey directly in the eye. Stacey's stomach was now growling. She felt like someone was playing on a big kettledrum inside her head.

"So I should be happy?" asked Stacey. "Right?"

"Well," said Roberta, "technically, you scored a victory. No one is going to bother you. But you do know that the council is a true reflection of public opinion. That means — the student body is evenly divided. I think it's safe to say that half the students are with you; half, against you."

Stacey began to move toward the auditorium.

"I can live with those results," said Stacey. "I'm not running for Homecoming Queen. I was never concerned with being Miss Popularity. I just want to play tennis."

"Well," said Roberta, "that's no problem. You'll certainly be able to continue playing tennis on the boys' team."

"Then I should be happy?" asked Stacey.

"That's right. You should be happy."

Stacey slept late on Sunday. When her parents suggested that she join them for some "social tennis" Stacey turned them down.

"Today's my lazy day," she said. "I just want to get my aching body to the beach. I want to get me some rays."

"Where did you pick up that expression?" her mother asked.

"I don't know, Mom. Where does anybody pick up any expression?"

"You're definitely in a grumpy mood," her mother said. "You'd *better* get to the beach."

Two hours later, Stacey was propped up on her elbows, squinting at a cool blue and green sail on the water. The sail was part of a windsurfer that belonged to the young German coach named Max. He was a hot topic of conversation among the girls at Neptune.

"Hey, Stace," said Michael, "you going to take off your T-shirt or are you afraid that you might get a tan?"

Stacey was wearing her "Eat Fish" shirt over a black bathing suit. Her face, arms, and legs were covered by sunblock. A floppy straw hat covered her hair.

"Mikey, don't you know that too much sun is bad for you? A tan may look pretty but it dries up the skin. Well, not the tan — but the sun. Get it?"

"Got it!"

"Good!"

Stacey's eyes scanned the beach. The surfers were in their customary area, like sea birds roosting in their watery nests. Wally Baxter was among them, working the long board with a balletic skill. Stacey had to admire his athletic ease.

The blond, ruggedly-built Max was showing off his windsurfing skills. A quartet of girls were huddled at the shore, watching him navigate his craft with and against the wind and the tide. Jackie Girard and Debby Klinger were part of this group.

So which one is Keith's girl? wondered Stacey. Both? Neither?

Some twenty yards down the beach, a familiar figure appeared, a wiry, brown-skinned young man carrying his surfboard. It was Stacey's solitary surfer. He was at that part of the beach between the high school crowd and the family crowd. So what's his story? mused Stacey. Does he have bad breath? Or maybe he just likes to surf and he doesn't need to party or socialize? Maybe he doesn't care what people think?

"Everyone needs friends," blurted out Stacey.

Michael rolled over on the sand and sat up.

"That's very profound," he said. "I've got an intellectual for a sister."

"Don't be sarcastic," said Stacey. "Just because you gave one brilliant concert doesn't make you a genius . . . or a wise guy."

Stacey stood up and walked toward the shore. Pam Hayward and Dave Kelly were preparing a windsurfer for the water. They looked up as Stacey approached and waved to her. Stacey thought of Roberta's words after the Student Council meeting — a reflection of public opinion!

"So half the beach crowd is for me," Stacey said to herself. "And half the crowd is against what I did. Well, that's life, I guess. Can't please everyone."

Pam and David offered to let Stacey try out the windsurfer. She quickly agreed. She needed to concentrate on something that was physically demanding. Her social life was not going to be resolved on this sunny Sunday afternoon. Once she had lifted the big blue and white sail out of the water, established her footing, gotten her grip, and guided the sail to get the maximum wind efficiency, Stacey's mind drifted away to thoughts of boys in general and Keith in particular. He was so nice to her, alternately gentle and stern, sensitive to her situation on the team. But regardless of the mystery of his girl friend or girl friends, Keith had shown no romantic interest in Stacey. That was a fact of life. But why should Stacey wait to be asked? Why must the boy initiate the date?

"As long as I know what I want or who I want," said Stacey, leaning away from the sail.

At that moment, she felt like taking the windsurfer far across the Atlantic, far from everyone.

Suddenly, there was Wally, paddling out to her on a yellow rubber raft. At the same time, the wind died down. In this whole wide ocean, thought Stacey, why must I be trapped with Wally Baxter?

She clutched at the handlebar, trying to keep the sail high and maintain her balance.

"Hey, Stacey, Orange Crush time coming up! Are we going?"

She leaned back, working the sail, trying to judge the new wind direction and keep her balance, all at the same time.

"Or are you waiting to hear from Keith?" shouted Wally.

"Oh come on, don't be ridiculous."

Well, she wouldn't be taking a solo flight across the sea, Stacey decided. And perhaps she *was* starting to talk to herself too much.

"I demand an answer," Wally shouted.

Stacey looked up at the clouds. They were sitting listlessly overhead, as if watching this ridiculous farce. She prayed that her instructor, Max, would come flying by in a motorboat and tug her away.

"I don't want to go to the Orange Crush," shouted Stacey. "I don't even care about the Orange Crush." Her voice sounded strident in the deadening calm of the ocean.

"If you don't say yes, I'll keep you out here forever," said Wally, playing. "But if you play your cards right, I'll get you back to shore."

"What do you mean, play my cards right?"

"Let me take you to the Orange Crush," insisted Wally.

"That's blackmail, Baxter."

Maybe I can swim to shore, thought Stacey

as desperation welled up inside her.

A slight breeze kicked up, causing her craft to pitch, rolling up and down, up and down. Stacey was feeling a little sick to her stomach. Suddenly there was a real wind and the windsurfer was churning like her stomach. She struggled with the sail and with the cross-bar. She fought to keep her feet balanced on the wet, slippery deck.

"Last chance to let me take you back to shore," taunted Wally. "Last chance to let me take you to the Orange Crush."

"All right already," cried Stacey. "All right. All right!"

Then she fell into the turbulent ocean as the craft overturned and the tall sail collapsed over. She swam quickly away, surfacing alongside Wally's boat. As she spit salt water out of her mouth, Stacey could hear Wally chortling and cheering.

"So we're definitely on for the Crush?" demanded Wally.

"Yes, yes, I did say yes," cried Stacey.

She flung her hands skyward and immediately sank beneath the waves. A moment later, she surfaced and swam out to her windsurfer.

So this is how some boys get their dates, thought Stacey. Entrapment!

Twelve

The following Friday, Coach Albertson and the team traveled south to Fort Lauderdale for the Sunshine Bowl. It was an opportunity for the smaller schools to compete and get exposure and experience. On the bus Stacey was accompanied by her father. There had been a family crisis, Michael was giving a concert that Saturday night. It was finally agreed Lucinda King would attend that event. Bill King wanted to take one of the two family cars. But Stacey wanted to ride with the team. The compromise had Bill on the bus with his daughter and the team.

Stacey settled herself next to the window, closed her eyes and imagined herself dancing wildly with Keith Flowers. Her hair was light and frizzy. She wore a shoulderless white dress that flared out as Keith spun her around and around the dance floor. At the same time that Stacey was dancing in her head, her father was engaged in a friendly discussion with Stan and Chuck Jones.

"So how do you like your daughter being on the team?" asked Chuck.

Bill King stretched his legs into the aisle. He smiled at the identical twins who were sitting across the way.

"Well, I was a little nervous at first," he admitted, "but I'm real proud of her. Always was. How about you boys? How do you feel?"

Stacey stopped her daydream dance with Keith. Now she was listening intently.

"We were also a little nervous at first," said Stan Jones.

"I still am," said Chuck, with a laugh. "She always beats me."

"But she's good," said Stan, "and that's the bottom line. Yeah, and she's good for the team."

Soon, Keith and Van joined the Jones brothers and Bill King in the back of the bus. They all got into a spirited discussion on sports. Stacey opened her eyes. Her dance would have to be deferred.

The minibus zoomed down the highway. The towns all looked alike, it seemed to Stacey. Used car lots, new car lots, restaurant chains selling tacos, fried chicken, and burgers.

"You can hardly see the beaches for the chickens and the cars," she said aloud.

Her father was preoccupied. He suddenly began talking about Stacey's need to make a good showing at the tournament, to attract a major tennis college, to shop around for a good coach.

"Dad, I'll get into a good school. I'll win my tournaments. But I'd like to have a normal life."

"I know what you're talking about," he said. "You discovered boys. You discovered dating. Well, don't forget that you're just a kid. Don't start getting involved with one boy."

"Fat chance," said Stacey.

Then she realized that Keith was sitting directly in front of her. Stacey hoped that he did not hear this conversation.

A few minutes later, Coach Albertson got the team together and announced that Keith and Van would play the two singles matches; the Jones brothers would play the doubles.

Stacey's heart sank to the soles of her tennis shoes. She figured her poor showing against Valdosta was the reason. She also knew that she had decisively won her next four matches and she and Keith had beaten Stan and Chuck in the intersquad doubles.

After the meeting broke up, Stacey and Keith remained in the back of the bus.

"So what are you thinking?" asked Keith. "You don't look happy."

"Maybe I should have taken my family's advice," grumbled Stacey, "and gone to a big tennis school down south. Life's not fair!"

"Whoever said that life was supposed to

159

be fair," said Keith. "Anyway, life in Neptune is a snap. You try surviving in the backwoods of Georgia. A big victory is when you get a decent crop, when the frost doesn't destroy half a year's work. Tennis is just a game."

"I didn't know you grew up on a farm in Georgia."

Keith stretched his long legs and stared out the window.

"Neptune's a big city," he whispered. "Stuff like the shopping mall and Hermosa Pier are like some kind of cotton candy heaven. Unreal!"

"Yeah," said Stacey. "Unreal. And tennis is . . . just a game."

She smiled at him.

"But it's the only game I know," she concluded, wistfully.

"You know," confided Keith, "as you've been getting better, I've been getting worse. I'm slow getting to the ball."

Stacey was pleased that he was opening up to her. She suggested he watch the ball more carefully as it came off the opponent's racquet, that he watch the other player's toss while he was receiving serve. She went on like this for some fifteen minutes, giving the attentive Keith the benefit of her years of playing experience and good coaching. Finally, he thanked her warmly and returned to his seat at the front of the bus.

Early Saturday morning, the Neptune

team made their entrance on two of the back courts. Neptune High did not have a great reputation as a tennis power but there was a sizeable crowd on hand to gape at Stacey King. She came out with two racquets tucked under her arm. Stacey was ready to play. She could only pray that Coach Albertson had a change of mind . . . or a change of heart.

"Well," said Stacey, "if I don't get to play, all the thrill seekers are going to be disappointed."

Coach Albertson snorted, then chuckled.

"Still," she continued, "I know that Keith and I can play excellent doubles. In fact. . . . "

"In fact," interrupted Albertson, "I know you guys can play better doubles than Stan and Chuck. But the brothers Jones would be devastated. Plus the fact that they have been winning. What the heck! Tennis is not that big a sport in Neptune!"

"It wasn't," said Stacey, "until I came on the team."

The Neptune team did not last past Saturday. Although Keith won his singles match, Van lost. The Jones boys were defeated in a hard-fought battle. Keith was particularly pleased with his playing and credited Stacey with giving him good advice.

"Hey champ," he called out, "my concentration was a hundred percent better, thanks to you."

Stacey felt a deep glow of satisfaction. As she walked slowly toward the clubhouse, she enjoyed the feeling of recognition, of approval, on a more personal level than she had ever felt before. But immediately a new sensation began gnawing its way within her. Keith was still number one. Now she realized, as if for the first time, that being number one was very important to her. Stacey frowned under the glaring sun. With a slight shudder, she understood her jealousy of Keith's success. She understood just how competitive she really was.

On Sunday, back in Neptune, Wally took Stacey on a canoe trip through the Blue Lagoon. As he paddled intently, he told her about the problems of getting a decent football scholarship. As he droned on and on, Stacey closed her eyes and tried to concentrate on the smell of wisteria, on the sound of the oar dipping into the cool water, on the gentle breeze caressing her upturned face. Suddenly she heard guitars and singing voices. The canoe came around a bend and there was Keith Flowers, sitting on a huge boulder, with Jackie Girard and Debby Klinger. They were all in bathing suits, playing guitars. Stacey was delighted.

"Hi guys," she shouted, "what's going on?"

"Nuts," shouted back Debby. "You discovered our secret rehearsal place."

"It's a public park," insisted Wally.

"We're rehearsing for the Orange Crush," Jackie said. "It's supposed to be a surprise. So don't you dare open your mouths — especially you, Wally Baxter."

"Guys don't gossip," boasted Wally.

"Oh yeah?" said Stacey. "Since when?"

Wally observed Stacey's admiring eyes focused on Keith.

"Come on," he said quickly. "It's time to go back." He started to back-paddle.

Stacey had one leg out of the canoe. She was ready to wade to shore. Instantly, there was a pushing and a pulling of the canoe. Wally kept trying to paddle away while Stacey was half-out, half-in. The canoe overturned, throwing them into the shallow water. Stacey was totally drenched, but she felt great.

"Don't worry about me, Wally Baxter," she laughed, "I'm just going to swim home."

"And what about me?" he said.

"You? You'll have to dry up."

Wally righted the canoe and paddled away furiously.

"Hey, champ," Keith said to Stacey, "I think you're finally starting to lighten up. You just had to get all wet to do it."

Stacey waded to the big boulder. She sat down heavily, then removed her tennis shoes and her white socks. She turned toward the sun, letting the rays begin the process of drying off her T-shirt and jeans.

"So this is the secret of Keith Flowers. . . ." began Stacey.

". . . and the Flower girls," said Keith. "Hey, that's a great name for the group."

"No, it's not," said Debby Klinger. "Too sexist."

"I agree," said Jackie Girard.

"And I agree," said Stacey King.

The semi-tropical sun dried out her clothes as Stacey lay back and listened to the music. She was observing yet another side of Keith. His singing and his guitar strumming were playful, but there was a brooding quality underneath. Finally the two girls put down their guitars. Keith sang country songs of Georgia springtimes, dusty roads, painfully lonely days and nights. He sang of a past that was far removed from the lawns, the canals, and the tennis courts of Neptune. And yet, to Stacey's eyes and ears, he carried his past with him. It was not far below that blue-eyed surface.

In the early evening, Keith drove Stacey home. Neither one said very much during the long drive. Stacey sat quietly in the car for a moment, then thanked Keith for a lovely time. She knew that it was more than just a "lovely time" but the right words didn't come easily. Perhaps, thought Stacey, I'm not ready to deal with the right words.

Later, when she was alone in her room, she called Wally and suggested that it might be best for both of them if they found other dates for the Orange Crush. Wally grumbled but Stacey persisted. She was already beginning the long process of finding out who she was — off the tennis courts.

Thirteen

Stacey got a new look. On the following Saturday afternoon, she stepped out of *Heads West*, nervously pleased with a hairdo that was considerably shorter than it had ever been before.

"Don't make it punk," she had warned Beverly, the number one stylist, beautician, and owner of the establishment.

And it wasn't punk. Certainly, there were no streaks of orange or vermillion. There was no jagged look. But the pony tail was gone. The long waves were gone. Beverly, chewing gum and talking all the while, had shaped it so that the hair was combed forward and to the side. It fell to just below Stacey's ears.

She got on her bike, then checked out her reflection in the store window. Not bad, she thought. I might even get to like it. But as she rode toward the King Pharmacy, Stacey was filled with giddy self-doubts.

Bill King was filling prescriptions in the

back room. He looked up, peering over his half-glasses and smiled.

"Very nice indeed," he said.

"Are you sure?" asked Stacey. "You're not just saying that?"

A moment later, Lucinda King was scrutinizing the new look.

"Does take some getting used to," she said. "But it frames your face nicely. At least, we can see your face."

Stacey was already getting bored with the subject of her own new hair style. Her head felt lighter — and she liked that feeling. More than that, she knew it was time for a change. She now realized she liked her new look, not only for itself, but because it was different. It certainly would be easy to manage. It would give her no problems on the tennis court.

"Well, I like it," she decided aloud.

"Good," said her mother. "That's all that counts. Feel free to ask our opinion any time."

The following evening Pam Hayward came over to see what *Heads West* had done to her friend. She immediately nodded her approval.

"Way to go, Stace. Now if we can just get you wearing brighter colors — if you can start wearing something besides tennis shorts and T-shirts, that will be a sure sign of progress."

"Very funny, Hayward. It so happens I have an extensive wardrobe of slacks and dresses and all that. I just save them for special occasions."

"Okay, girl, then it's time for more 'special occasions.' "

They took a long walk around the neighborhood, talking about all the events of the past three months. Stacey told Pam about the Blue Lagoon experience.

"Keith sounds very cool," Pam decided.

"Not cool," said Stacey. "Shy. I think that's his big secret. He's a shy guy."

They were now strolling through a new part of town, a neighborhood of expensive ranch-houses, swimming pools and U-shaped driveways.

"You ever notice," said Stacey, "how nobody walks the streets of Neptune. It's only seven o'clock, but you'd think it was a ghost town. Where is everybody?"

"Watching television, I guess," said Pam.

Suddenly they heard the dull, rhythmic wacking of tennis balls. It was coming from a backyard, from someone's private court, complete with arc lights.

"Do you believe this?" whispered Pam. "High Society comes to Neptune."

The two girls tiptoed through a long driveway and there, behind a sprawling ranch house, was a brightly-illuminated tennis court. Sally Llewellyn and Van Larsen were having a furious work-out. Play immediately came to a dead halt as Stacey and Pam approached the wire fence that enclosed the court. Sally looked flustered. Stacey looked flustered. Stacey couldn't tell if the red face was from all the court activity or from embarrassment.

"Please don't stop on our account," said Pam.

"Hi, everybody," said Stacey. "This is a great court. Who does it belong to?"

Van walked over to a small white table and poured himself a glass of orange juice from a green plastic pitcher.

"My dad built it," he said. "Didn't cost very much."

"I'll bet," said Pam.

Sally was now bouncing a ball impatiently with her racquet.

"Let's go, Van," she said.

Van flashed a big smile at Stacey, then he finished his drink.

"I'm getting ready for my next intersquad match," he said, pointing his finger at Stacey. "So I want to know what it feels like to play against a good woman player."

"You'll find out on Tuesday," said Stacey, without batting an eyelash.

Pam did a double-take. She had never heard her friend speak in such a forthright manner. It seemed to go with her streamlined look.

"Listen, King," said Van, "whoever wins on Tuesday moves up a notch. I mean, you have a chance at being the new number two player."

"And do you think you really have a chance of being number one?" asked Stacey.

Van laughed loudly.

"I think we both have a chance of being number one," he said. "You agree, don't you? Unless you don't think you have a chance against Keith Flowers?"

For a moment, Stacey could only tap her sneakers on the soft grass.

"I just take it one match at a time," she said, finally.

Sally looked flustered as she continued to bounce the tennis ball.

"Give him a good workout, Sally," said Stacey. "Keep the ball deep to his backhand."

"I'm just doing what you've always done," said Sally. "Working out with the boys to improve my game."

"I think that's great," said Stacey. "I really do."

There was a moment of tension as Van walked back onto the court to receive service.

Pam was tugging at Stacey's sleeve.

"Sorry we can't stay and watch you guys," she shouted. "But Stacey and I are studying together. We were just taking a little break."

All of a sudden, Sally put down her racquet and walked quickly over to Stacey.

"Listen," she said, "I know you think I'm responsible for that Gender Cross-Over debate. But I really had nothing to do with it."

Stacey's mouth fell open. That was the last thing in the world she expected to hear.

"Sally Llewellyn, I'm not going to call you a liar," said Stacey in an even voice, "but you stand the risk of being frozen in this spot for the rest of your natural life if you keep spouting those crazy words of yours."

"What are you talking about?" asked Sally, reaching out to touch Stacey's arm.

Stacey held out her hand, keeping the girl at arm's length.

"I've put up with a lot of nonsense from you," said Stacey, "and frankly I'm sick of it. And I'm sick of you."

Van Larsen clutched his tennis racquet to his chest. A thin smile played on his lips.

"I've always been your friend," protested Sally. "Ask anyone."

"I don't have to ask anyone," said Stacey. "I remember, after my date with Chuck Jones, when you sweetly volunteered the information that he called me a tennis machine."

"I just wanted you to know. . . . "

"You just wanted to humiliate me," Stacey said. "There was no need to tell me. You had to know I'd be hurt."

"What about the parties I invited you to?" asked Sally. "I wanted you to be part of the group."

"So you made me feel like an outsider," said Stacey. "I don't forget what people say to me. And you said, ' . . . if you find a boy, bring him to the party.' Well, you knew darn well I wouldn't find a boy. I didn't know any boys; not then. So I went to that B.Y.O.B. party. I was the only girl without a date. And you were all dressed up, you and Pam, and everybody. And I was in my little girl's tennis outfit. 'Cause nobody told me I *had* to bring a boy. Nobody told me it was a dressy occasion."

"That was my fault, too," whispered Pam.

Stacey's eyes were still riveted on the fidgety Sally Llewellyn.

"And now," shouted Stacey, "you have the nerve to lie to my face. Van told me that you got a friend of yours to introduce the Gender Cross-Over resolution."

"Van said that?" gasped Sally.

"I confess," said Van. "I admit the deed."

"And," continued Stacey, "you were also jealous that Van took me out. Well, Sally Llewellyn, you got any more friendly words for me? Because I sure don't have any more friendly words for you."

Stacey grabbed Pam's hand and pulled her away and they strode purposefully away.

On Monday afternoon Van Larsen had a grueling workout with Keith Flowers. Afterwards, they took showers and dressed quickly.

"Good luck tomorrow," said Keith, matter-of-factly.

"Who are you wishing 'good luck?' " asked Van. "Your sympathies are clearly with the young lady."

"Hey man, what are you talking about?"

Their voices echoed slightly off the tiled walls. It made for an eerie sound in the empty locker room.

"I mean," said Van, "you and Stacey have

171

a little mutual admiration society. You coach her. She coaches you. You encourage her. She encourages you. Very cozy. Why don't you just start dating her and get it over with?"

Keith looked long and hard at his teammate, then slowly put on his jacket.

"First of all, don't tell me who I should be dating. Jackie occupies most of my time."

"And Debby occupies some of your time?" asked Van, with a sneer.

He started to put on his own team jacket, then changed his mind and folded it over his arm.

"And Stacey occupies none of my time," said Keith, "off the court."

"Yeah," said Van, "but she occupies a lot of your head. Hey, don't you know what's going on with you? Is she your coach, your pupil, your teammate, or your next girlfriend?"

Keith began to comb his hair, slowly, carefully, affecting a nonchalance as he avoided Van's hard stare.

"I think," said Keith, "that Stacey has a good crack at being the number two player on this team."

He pocketed his comb. Then he picked up his books and his tennis bags and walked out the door. Keith was disturbed. Maybe Van's questions were right on. What were his feelings toward Stacey?

"Just friends," he muttered to himself. "Just friends."

Fourteen

Tuesday morning Stacey was very meticulous as she packed her tennis clothes. She thought long and hard, then decided on a pale blue shirt with navy blue stripes running across the shoulders and down the sleeves. She selected a matching navy blue pair of shorts. Then she chose her favorite wristband, solid crimson, and placed it in the right pocket of her tennis shorts. The ritual calmed her. She was out to get Van Larsen, to wipe the smirking smile off his face. Yet Stacey did not want to become so emotionally upset that she would turn into a wild woman. She did not believe that athletes should engage in temper tantrums or violent outbursts. She only wanted to play her kind of game.

At three o'clock, under an overcast sky, she did just that. Playing an aggressive serve-and-volley game, committing few errors, she dispatched an increasingly agitated Van Larsen, 7-6, 7-5, 6-1. Coach Albertson beamed down at her.

"I'm real proud of you," he said. "You justified my faith in you. Young lady, I think you can go all the way. You've got a bright future in this sport."

Marcel Philippe extended his small hand and congratulated her. Stan and Chuck, in unison, mumbled, "Nice work." Van took Stacey aside, breathing heavily, and shook his head.

"Got to hand it to you," he said, "you did a number on me. Good is good. And you're good. Hey, no hard feelings from this boy. I'll even take you to another Wendell Vose concert.

"Thanks, Van, I appreciate that."

Life is sure full of surprises, thought Stacey, as she watched Van begin the long walk to the locker room.

The biggest surprise was Keith's reaction. His eyes were downcast, a stony expression was on his face when Albertson announced Stacey and Keith would play each other on Thursday for the number one ranking. Stacey waited for the smile or nod of approval she usually received from Keith after a good match, but he avoided her questioning gaze and hurried away with Jackie Girard.

Stacey grew more and more disturbed as she rode home on her bike. The music from her Walkman radio did not help. She was exhausted from her difficult match with Van. Stacey was emotionally drained — the joy of winning, that "up" feeling, was tempered by Keith's cold behavior. Was he jealous? Was he so competitive after all that he had no room in his heart for a simple "congratulations?" Stacey was preoccupied with these difficult questions and with the rock and roll music blasting in her ears. She didn't hear the honking of the van behind her. The driver was trying to pass Stacey, who was mindlessly riding along the middle of the street. Finally, she heard the blaring horn. She swerved to the right, allowing the agitated driver to pass.

Stacey hopped off the bike and switched off the radio.

"I think I need a break," she said aloud.

She pedalled quickly to Pam's house. Luckily, her best friend was home. They sat by the canal, listening to music and not saying much. After ten minutes, Stacey confessed that she was worried.

"I could see that, a mile away," said Pam. "Did you lose?"

"Lose what?"

"Your match, dummy," Pam said. "That little game we play with a ball and a racquet. Remember? Wow!"

"Oh, no," Stacey answered absentmindedly. "I beat Van."

"You don't look overjoyed. Hey, what's going on?"

Stacey described Keith's behavior. It all seemed so senseless.

"You don't really know the guy," suggested

Pam. "He's just one of those cool athletes with a blond smile. Just another pretty face."

"I was sure he was different," said Stacey. "But he had the kind of pouting expression that I'd see in Wally Baxter."

Pam fixed Stacey with a deep, questioning look.

"Okay," said Stacey, "so I've got a crush on the guy. And when I found out that Jackie and Debby were just friends, I really thought I had a chance. Boy, am I ever dumb. I don't know anything."

"Well, you have to start somewhere," sighed Pam. "Last year, you weren't dating at all. At least, you're out there."

"Where?" asked Stacey. "Nowhere!"

From the transistor radio, a rough female voice was singing loud and strong.

"Walk away, walk away from the table/ when love's no longer being served. . . ."

"Dumb lyrics," said Pam. "But they make their point."

Stacey stood up and wiped the grass off her jeans.

"I really thought I was Miss Tennis Queen. Keith was so nice to me in Fort Lauderdale. Van took me to a concert. Wally begged to take me to the Orange Crush. Why? Because I'm Miss Tennis Machine. I'm debated in the Student Council. I'm like the first woman astronaut. First female into space! Hah! Pam, maybe it's time for me to blast off."

"Girl, what are you talking about?"

"I'm playing hookey tomorrow," whispered Stacey. "I'm cutting classes; cutting tennis practice. I'm taking my tapes and my books and I'm running away to my little old shack on Runaway Beach. I've had it."

"Pretty drastic move," said Pam.

Her dark eyes tried to see inside her friend's mind. Was Stacey serious? Pam could not advise her long-time friend. No one could.

"Get that worried expression off your face," said Stacey. "I'm just running away for the day. I'll tell my folks that I'll be home a little late for dinner. I'll call Albertson and say that I'm not feeling so hot. Pam, I need a break. I need time alone, to think. I don't know what to make of Keith. I don't know what to make of myself. I'm fifteen, going on . . . early retirement! Tennis was not fun today. Nothing was fun today. And there's got to be more to life than trying to be the greatest tennis player in Neptune, Florida."

Early the following morning, Stacey was pedaling along the service road that led to Runaway Beach. Her cassette player, her eight favorite tapes and two books of poetry were in her backpack, along with two bathing suits, two towels, assorted fresh fruit . . . and a tube of sun block.

Keith was upset when Stacey did not show up for practice. He couldn't accept Coach Albertson's explanation that Stacey had phoned in, saying she was sick. At three o'clock, he asked to be excused.

"What's your problem?" asked Albertson.

"My back's starting to act up," Keith lied. "I'd like to rest it."

"What's going on here?" said the coach. "Am I going to lose my entire squad? Who's going to be next?"

"I'll be fine tomorrow," Keith promised.

Albertson dismissed him with a wave of his hand. Keith tried not to run too quickly to the locker room. But once the door was closed, he hurriedly got dressed. Then he drove quickly to Stacey's home.

Fifteen minutes later, Keith was standing in front of the white stucco house. He rang the bell, waited, and rang again. Then he pounded on the heavy oak door. Finally Keith ran around to the backyard. He shouted Stacey's name. For a few seconds, he waited. But the only sound he heard was the faint chirping of cicadas on the green lawn.

Keith jumped into his car and drove to Pam Hayward's house. Fortunately for him, she was just getting home from her practice session.

"Where's your friend?" asked Keith.

"Which one?"

"Come on, Pam, don't play games. Where's Stacey?"

Pam bit her lip, then shrugged her shoulders.

"Something's wrong," insisted Keith. "She wasn't at the courts. She's not home. I know she's upset. Don't ask me why."

"Why?"

"Don't ask," shouted Keith. "Just tell me where she is."

Finally, Pam revealed that Stacey was at her family house in Runaway Beach. It was on the tip of her tongue to add that her friend wanted to be alone. But when she studied Keith's face, she realized he was genuinely concerned. That was a healthy sign.

"The house isn't far from the surfers' beach. It's a motley colored kind of shack. Looks like a good wind will blow it down."

"I'll find it," said Keith. "I'll find her."

Keith drove the seven miles to the beach. Then he began running along the shore. He didn't question his own agitated behavior. Keith only knew that he had to see Stacey and talk to her. Suddenly there she was, running toward him, a golden brown and white figure in the distance.

Stacey's mouth fell open when she spotted Keith.

"What are you doing here?" she gasped.

They stood facing one another, breathing heavily. A strong sea breeze ruffled Stacey's hair. Her large T-shirt billowed like a sail on a windsurfer.

"The question is," said Keith, "what are you doing here?"

"I'm trying to lighten up," said Stacey, finally, managing a smile.

They exchanged long, questioning looks. Neither was ready to express real feelings. Neither understood the mutual attraction that was drawing them together. So they sat on the sand and watched a lone surfer. He kept getting knocked over by the waves or losing his balance. Stacey now recognized him as the solitary surfer who seemed to spend all his waking hours in the water.

"I do admire his determination," said Stacey.

"Yeah," said Keith. "Not much technique but a lot of heart."

They began talking about their upcoming match on Thursday. One of them would emerge as number one.

"I'm a little nervous," admitted Keith. "Or maybe a lot nervous. That's why I was so cold yesterday. I'm sorry. I never thought of you as a rival before. I never thought of myself as a hard-nosed competitor. I'm not sure I like the picture. I'd like us to be friends."

And then he added, "Even if I lose."

"I'm glad you said that. I feel the same way. I mean, whatever happens on Thursday, I'd like us to be friends." Then Stacey added, with a shy smile, "Even if I win."

They sat close together on the windswept beach, looking out to sea. Stacey did not feel cold. But she wanted to huddle against him. Keith had his legs up, his muscular arms over his knees, as he spoke of family pressure.

"My dad wants me to be a world-class player. I don't know if it's worth all the hassles."

Stacey observed him with a sideways glance. She saw her own conflicts and problems in his eyes: dreams of glory, ambition, a driving, competitive personality. How could their warm feelings for each other be expressed if they were rivals on a tennis court?

An hour later, Keith drove Stacey back to town, to the King Pharmacy. Michael was alone at a booth, having gone through his own rough workout in a rehearsal hall.

"Hey, Stace, hey, Keith, come on over. I'll buy you a lemonade."

The young men shook hands. Keith slid into the booth alongside Michael. Stacey smiled at them.

"Maybe I should have been a tennis player," said Michael. "At least I wouldn't have to deal with temperamental conductors."

"Hey, friend," said Keith, "I'll switch places with you. Then you can deal with super-sensitive athletes. It's a no-win situation."

They laughed knowingly, exchanging looks of recognition and understanding. Stacey watched them with growing interest. She noticed how easily Keith and Michael got along, each openly curious about the other, each attentive and solicitous to the other's concerns. She wondered if perhaps boys viewed girls as some kind of a threat, even if the girls weren't hot-shot athletes.

"Hey, you guys, I want to ask you both a question!"

Michael and Keith turned away from each

other and looked at Stacey across the high-polished table.

"I have a question," announced Stacey. "What's the worst thing that could happen if I turned out to be the number one player on the boys' tennis team?"

"I know you're really asking me," said Keith, suddenly grave and low-voiced.

"So what's your gut feeling?" asked Stacey.

"As of this moment," said Keith, "I'd think of myself of a loser, as number two. I never thought about these things before, not since you got me thinking about them back at the beach. But I'd . . . I'd look on myself as a failure. And I guess . . . I'd hold you responsible. 'Cause you'd be the one who beat me."

"Well," said Stacey slowly, "I asked the question. And I got the answer. I'm not sure I liked the answer but I got it anyway."

Fifteen

Stacey and Pam strolled across the grass and onto the number one tennis court. Without a word being spoken, they proceeded to warm up. It was one o'clock on a hot Thursday afternoon. Stacey's match with Keith was about to begin.

"Whenever you guys are ready," said Albertson to Keith and Stacey. "Make your own line calls. If there's a dispute, I'll be the final judge."

Stacey nodded to Keith in a friendly gesture — but he was unable to look her in the eye. He appeared to be preoccupied.

In the first set, both players made numerous errors. They were tentative and distracted. During the one minute rest periods, Stacey couldn't help but feel saddened at Keith's grim face.

This game is definitely not a fun sport, she thought. Not today, anyway.

Halfway through the first set, Keith abandoned his usual cool, laid-back game. He became more aggressive as Stacey continued to flub easy shots. Keith won the first set, 6-3.

Before the start of the second set, Stacey draped a big white towel over her head.

From the grandstand, it appeared that Stacey was praying. Actually, she needed to cut herself off from the visual distraction of Keith, from her family, and from the others. Stacey vowed to do nothing more daring than to keep the ball in play and try to hit deeply to the baseline. Before the match, she'd had no strategy. Now she had a strategy and it worked. Stacey was sending Keith a message that she was prepared to stay out there all day, if necessary. Now Keith began to fall apart as he pushed for quick winners. He took more chances, tried for low percentage shots in his impatience to put an end to each point as quickly as possible. Stacey, on the other hand, played a disciplined, steady-as-a-rock game. She only flashed her old aggressiveness when Keith hit a weak shot. Then Stacey moved in swiftly and put the ball away for an easy winner. She took the second set, 6-2.

Stacey continued her game plan and took the third set, 6-4. Now she was only one set away from victory. Keith began to make spectacular shots. Stacey returned them all. As she grew more confident, he became more frustrated. By the end, she had beaten Keith, 6-3. But there was no tossing of racquets, no clenched fists to the sky, no falling on knees, no jumping over the net. Instead, the two players approached each other. Their hands reached out across the net and clasped each other for a fleeting moment. Now their eyes made contact. Between them was the undeniable truth of who each of them was — not winner, not loser, but friends of a very unique kind. Their eyes indicated a recognition of each other's uniqueness.

Coach Albertson had a quizzical expression on his face.

"Okay, Stacey King," he said, "I guess you're number one on the boys' team. Umm, I mean, the tennis . . . heck, you know what I mean. Congratulations, kid. You're number one."

Stacey wrapped a fresh towel around her neck. She tugged at Keith's damp shirt and pulled him toward her. Her moment of elation had passed. What mattered now was that Keith not be destroyed, that his sense of himself be salvaged and strengthened. Her heart truly went out to Keith, with all of his fears and defensiveness, she cared for him.

"You know, Coach," said Stacey, "I really and truly don't care who's number one."

Keith was looking intently at Stacey, as if for the first time. There was a special attentiveness and respect in his eyes. He put his tired, sweaty arm around Stacey.

"Coach," he said, "I care. And she deserves the number one ranking. She also deserves my respect."

That night Keith and Stacey went for a long walk along Pelican Beach. Stacey felt as if she could stroll forever on the soft sand. A full moon illuminated the darkly sparking waters.

"I have to tell you something," said Keith. "Actually — I mean to say — the point is. . . ."

He took off his white shoes and began walking along the flat, muddy shoreline. Stacey removed her open-toed shoes and ran after him. The ground was cool and pleasant under her feet.

"Go ahead and finish your sentence," she said. "It's okay. You can talk. I really want to hear what you have to say."

Now they were walking hand-in-hand. Stacey had no sense of time passing. She knew that Keith would speak when he was ready.

"I like you," he said, finally. "Okay? Okay! I like you."

"Well, I like you, too," said Stacey.

"Well, I could have told you that before," said Keith. "I always knew I liked you. Even when your hair was long!"

"Oh yeah?" she said with mock sarcasm. "It took you long enough to notice my new hairdo. Besides, I always knew I liked you."

"Oh yeah," said Keith, mimicking her voice. "Well, I liked you first."

"Yeah, yeah, yeah," said Stacey. "I liked you first."

"We're really two mature adults, aren't

we?" asked Keith, as they fell to the sand, laughing. Then they kissed, a sweet, tender kiss, under a full Florida moon.

Later, they strolled over to Hermosa Pier, to the Orange Crush. They danced on the pier, then ran away to dance on the sand. Still later, they went swimming in the warm ocean, laughing and joking with each other. They were no longer tennis rivals. It didn't matter that Stacey was number one; not to her, not to Keith. They were simply two people who had become fond of each other as they had gone through some intense experiences. Stacey's eyes were glistening brightly.

"I tell you, Flowers, we're going to be one terrific mixed doubles team!"

He kissed her, then held her hand as they strolled back toward Hermosa Pier.

"You're the only tennis player I've ever wanted to kiss," said Keith, grinning broadly.

Stacey burst out laughing.

"I should hope so. Actually I feel the same way about you."

The words spilled out of her. Suddenly she grew silent.

"Is it okay if we don't talk for a while?" asked Stacey. "I'm feeling a little scared. I'm not even sure what I'm feeling. Scared — happy — it's all mixed up inside me.

"I understand," said Keith.

They could hear the dance music coming from the Orange Crush party. It shattered the silence, growing louder and louder.

"It's been a crazy year," said Stacey, finally. "All my life, it's just been tennis, tennis, and more tennis. And then I started to date and...."

"You don't have to say anything."

"A person has a right to change her mind, doesn't she? Well, now I want to talk. Keith, I like being with you. With or without the Orange Crush, with or without tennis, I like being with you."

"I feel the same way," he said, putting his arms tightly around her and kissing her again and again.

"Air!" cried Stacey. "I need air! Now I understand the expression: 'He took my breath away.'"

Suddenly they were interrupted by Jackie Girard and Debby Klinger.

"Our public is waiting," yelled Debby. "Come on!"

Keith, Debby, and Jackie sang for the boisterous, enthusiastic crowd, and Stacey King applauded louder than anyone. She was especially applauding for Keith. And then Keith put down his guitar and applauded for his new, mixed doubles partner — for the very special, for the number one, Stacey King.